THIS TIME FOREVER

FROM THIS DAY FORWARD
BOOK 3

DARA GIRARD

ISBN: 978-1-949764789

This Time Forever

Published by ILORI Press Books

ILORI PRESS BOOKS, LLC

P.O. Box 10332

Silver Spring, MD 20914

www.iloripressbooks.com

BOOKS BY DARA GIRARD

Duvall Sisters

The Glass Slipper Project

Taming Mariella

A Reluctant Hero

The Black Stockings Society

Power Play

A Gentleman's Offer

Body Chemistry

Round the Clock

Return of the Black Stockings Society

Playing for Keeps

After Hours

A Private Affair

Just One Look

Private Lessons

The Main Attraction

Ladies of the Pen

Words of Seduction

Pages of Passion

Beneath the Covers

Henson Series

Table for Two

Gaining Interest

Careless Rapture

Dangerous Curves

Familiar Stranger

It Happened One Wedding

Unexpected Pleasure

Midnight Promise

Sweet Temptation

Always and Forever

Truly Yours

Say Yes

Picture Perfect

By My Side

Clifton Sisters

The Sapphire Pendant

The Amber Stone

The Emerald Ring

Fortune Brothers

A Tempting Proposal

A Seductive Arrangement

An Unforgettable Moment

From This Day Forward

The Language of Flowers

Sooner or Later

This Time Forever

Novels

Honest Betrayal

The Daughters of Winston Barnett

Remember My Name

Illusive Flame

Winterwood Lane

Promise Me

This Changes Everything

Sparks

Piece of Cake

Best Laid Plans

Her Tender Touch

Dream of Me

1

———

It was a perfect day for a disaster.

The spring sun sat high in the sky highlighting the fashionably dressed wedding guests who stood outside the church unaware of the invisible storm clouds gathering strength.

But Catherine, better known as Cat, Kayode wasn't fooled as she stood at the base of the concrete steps. Not by the brightly colored outfits and artistically styled, colorful geles, proudly worn on the women's' heads. Not by the happy chatter and laughter. And especially not by the beautiful brown skinned woman dressed in a beaded white wedding dress who held a large bouquet in a grip so tight Cat was surprised the stems didn't snap, causing the bright blossoms to topple to the ground like a head sliced off at the guillotine.

She was certain no one else noticed the bride's steely grip or intense gaze. But Cat noticed these things because she was always aware when disaster was going to strike.

And it was going to strike today.

In a few minutes. Maybe even seconds.

And there was nothing anyone could do to stop it.

But as disasters went Cat knew this was to going to be a spectacular one.

The only thing missing was ring side seats and a tub of butter flavored popcorn.

Cat wasn't a big boxing fan (she preferred pro wrestling, don't judge) but she could easily imagine an announcer saying:

In this corner at 5'7 and 135 pounds we have Gwen the reigning, undefeated champion whose sucker punch could fell an elephant and in this corner just shy of 5'3 weighing 155 pounds we have Maya who's never won a match but refuses to stay down.

Cat's two eldest sisters were always at each other's throat and in spite of what the rumors said about Maya being a troublemaker, (rumors usually started by their mother or Gwen herself), Gwen was usually the one to instigate their sisterly spats.

Ever since her half-sister, Maya, had come to live with the Kayodes when she was fourteen years old (displacing Gwen as the eldest sister. A dethroning she'd never forgiven Maya for) there had been an uneasiness within their sisterly ranks.

Although Gwen was their mother's favorite (undisputed, uncontested) and Maya clearly wasn't (evidenced by how their mother had abandoned her until her own mother, Maya's grandmother, had died and could no longer care for Maya, forcing her to live with them); Gwen succeeded at everything, while Maya had more failures than a hive had bees. Gwen still couldn't stop being in competition with her. The environment had grown so bad that Maya had been forced to leave at nineteen years old only to return in disgrace nearly twenty years later because she'd lost her job and apartment. But that humiliation still wasn't enough to satisfy Gwen's ego.

It held an insatiable craving for more, like a starved zombie needing brains.

The beautiful bride not only craved the attention of everyone who had come to celebrate her wedding, but she also needed to show that she was the best.

She was going to shame Maya. Not only because she was upset by the simple ankara dress Maya had chosen to wear, instead of donning the elaborate lace golden and red *aso ebi* the entire family ensemble was supposed to, but because Maya existed as their mother's first born and for that Gwen would make her pay.

By tossing her flowers.

Knowing Maya hated attention and hated flowers even more. Knowing that at thirty-seven years old and unemployed, Maya was already seen as the pitiful Kayode sister and Gwen wasn't.

Cat glanced towards the parking lot with longing, eager for the event to end so they could all jump in their vehicles, go to the reception and eat, which was the only thing she looked forward to today. She then sent a quick glance at her other sister, Ava, who looked worried but kept her sweet face as composed as possible. She was the next one to please their parents with a suitable profession and a well-chosen fiancé.

Since she couldn't make eye contact with Ava, and warn her about what was about to happen, Cat sighed and returned her gaze to the bride. She steeled herself, ready to see Gwen spitefully toss the bouquet at poor Maya because Maya was to be pitied.

And that's where Cat envied her eldest sister a little. Not that she wanted to be pitied, but on the other hand no one ever thought of her. Gwen would never think to toss the bouquet at Cat.

Because she was the invisible sister.

People would no sooner pity Cat than a well-pampered pet.

And that's exactly how Cat felt dressed in the outfit her sister had chosen for them. She felt like a lizard forced into frills—utterly ridiculous. She was plain faced anyway and the colors and cut only seemed to emphasis everything her mother despaired about her, except for the fact she looked a decade younger than her actual age.

Aside from her lack of looks, which her three sisters all seemed to have gotten in spades, she had no hips, no waist, skinny arms and legs and the same bust size she'd had since she was twelve. She resisted the urge to take off her gele and loosen one of the thick—but tight!—box braids she'd managed to stuff underneath.

If Gwen had any tact, or even a modicum of respect for her sisters, she would have tossed the bouquet at Cat. But nobody expected Cat to get married or to have a life of her own. She was too homely and useful to the family for that possibility. Her parents saw her as their retirement and had been grooming her for that role for years (making sure she was too busy for friends or a social life; instead filling her time with afterschool activities such as helping with the cloth and dress shop and the two consignment stores that the family owned, as well as running errands for both her parents and sisters). She'd once had a brief reprieve when they'd allowed her to attend college, but it felt far in the past and a future of duty lay before her.

A duty that likely wouldn't end with her parents' passing because then she'd be designated as the maidenly aunt sent to live with one of her sisters and look after their children, possibly even their grandchildren. She was never meant to have a life of her own.

And she hadn't fought against that fate.

And at twenty-nine she wouldn't fight now.

Cat watched with a resigned malaise as Gwen tossed the bouquet in the air, making sure it was directed at Maya. Cat suppressed a yawn and waited.

She bet that Maya would grab the flowers then toss them back with the force of a javelin thrower.

But to her surprise Maya didn't do that.

Instead she ran. She ran as if the bouquet was a grenade; shoving people out of the way like a tiny linebacker as she tried to make her escape.

That's when Cat realized it would be a bigger disaster than she'd imagined.

Cat, in all her wild imaginings, would never have pictured the sight of Maya shoving her nemesis, Keeden Adesina, in front of a car. A car that would hit the poor man with enough force to make him bounce before he hit the ground.

And lay motionless.

For a brief moment—unbidden, unwanted—Bryant Meadows's face flashed through Cat's mind. Her heart constricted as she thought about the pain Keeden's best friend would face. He'd feel more anguish than even Keeden's father would. She thought of how devastation would shadow his usually bright brown eyes, how the news would turn down the corners of his ever present smile. She wondered who would deliver the news to him that...

But no... Keeden was alive.

Cat released a breath she hadn't known she'd been holding and allowed herself to observe the chaotic incident from a respectable distance. And the thought of Bryant disappeared, although she was annoyed that it had come to her in the first place. The man had no place in her thoughts. But she knew he was the kind of man who went where he wanted to. And had made unwanted appearances in her life and mind longer than she cared to admit.

After a few moments, Cat's curiosity got the better of her and she made her way forward.

She wasn't one of the first on the scene, but she was one of the few unafraid; making sure she was visible in case anyone needed her.

She watched the doctors and nurses (easily abundant in a gathering of Nigerian-Americans) take over before they started to argue about who was more suited to perform which task and then began to toss around degrees and alma maters as if they were at a quiz show.

Maya quickly took charge, like a general taking order of a rowdy troop of new recruits. Cat could easily see her in the role she'd held for many years as an art professor getting students to pay attention in spite of her small size.

She saw all the possible ways Maya could win them over and become the hero of this fiasco if given a chance.

Unfortunately, it might prove an impossible feat since Maya not only hated Keeden, but he was also an Adesina, one of the Kayode family's longest respected family friends. A bond that stretched generations. Smoothing over this debacle would take a lot of diplomatic cunning that Maya didn't have. But it would be interesting to watch how it would play out.

"What is wrong with you?" someone asked her in an urgent whisper.

So many things, Cat wanted to reply before she reluctantly turned.

2

"Why?" Cat said, meeting Ava's gaze with amusement. Her sister was as sweet as caramel taffy and attractive in all the ways that mattered.

"You're smiling like you're enjoying this."

Cat shrugged in no mood to deny it. "I am."

"This is a disaster."

An absolutely beautiful one. Better than she could have hoped for. "Serves Gwen right."

"But poor Keeden," Ava said near tears. "Stop smiling."

She couldn't help herself. "No one notices me, except you." And that silenced her sister as she knew it would because they both knew Cat was right.

"Doesn't matter," Ava said ever the diplomat. "Stop smiling. We're lucky his best friend Bryant isn't here."

This time Cat didn't feel like agreeing with her, annoyed that she'd thought about Bryant at all. She glanced past Ava and paused when she saw another sight that, while not as terrible as Keeden on the ground, may soon prove just as bad. She had to bite back another grin. Ava would have no tolerance for it. Cat knew she'd have to address what she'd seen soon but decided to wait. "Might do them both good," she said.

Ava frowned. "You have a sick way of looking at things."

Cat wagged her finger as if correcting a child. "Different. Not sick. And instead of worrying about me, you should worry about him." She nodded to Folu, Ava's fiancé, who stood as frozen as a man who'd been visited by a ballroom full of ghosts.

"You'd better catch him before he faints."

Cat bit back a grin pleased by her sister's rare look of annoyance. "It was one time," Ava said but Cat remembered many more times than the one where Folu screamed when a little frog had jumped out of a box in the garage they were organizing and then used Ava as a shield as if the little creature would leap up and devour him.

"We all have our flaws," Ava said in a prim voice she'd practiced for years. "We're not all fearless like you."

"I'm hardly fearless," Cat said ignoring the sting of her sister's criticism, "but I wouldn't use you as a shield either. I know Dai wouldn't."

The mention of Ava's best friend got the desired effect, Ava's face lit up and the mixture of annoyance and sadness disappeared before the ever present polite mask settled back in place. "Folu is not Dai."

"I'd no sooner compare a puddle with an ocean."

Ava shot her a look. "Folu is not Dai," she repeated.

"I know," Cat dutifully replied.

"He was hugging me for support."

It was painful watching her sister clutching at straws but Ava had to protect the reputation of her intended because although Cat found Folu as attractive as limp lettuce, Ava had invested years into eventually becoming his wife and nothing would dissuade her from that chosen path. Although Cat hoped something would, which was why she kept mentioning the garage incident. "He was hiding behind you like a—"

Ava held up her hand. "That's enough," she said in a tone that let Cat know she wouldn't indulge anymore. "Let me go check on him."

"Don't forget the smelling salts," Cat called after her.

To no surprise her sister ignored her.

Cat had no interest in seeing how her sister placated the man she was determined to marry, so she turned her attention back to the main event.

She saw Maya comforting the Old Woman. Lena Oluwa was really only a teenager but came across as much older so she'd earned the nickname. Except now, in spite of her tall height, stylish wig and contacts she looked like the lost, devastated fourteen year old she actually was. Lena was close to both Keeden and Bryant. Cat briefly imagined what she'd say to the young woman but she wasn't good at comforting people, and no one expected such a gesture from her anyway, so although Maya looked like a hen trying to comfort a flamingo, it seemed right to leave them alone.

Instead, crossing the semi-circle of people, Cat made her way over to her mother but halted when she saw her mother lean towards her husband and whisper words Cat couldn't hear.

But she could read them on her mother's beautiful lips.

Words that made her heart turn cold. Her mother, their mother, had said, "Shame it wasn't Maya."

3

———

From hell into heaven one bite at a time.

Cat briefly closed her eyes as she enjoyed another canapé, feeling as if she'd slipped into a parallel universe where there were no sibling rivalries, no cruelly callous words, no pathetic fiancés, no car accidents and family drama.

Cat swallowed then looked around the ballroom as most wedding reception guests (those only invited to the reception and not the wedding since the church had been too small) enjoyed themselves blithely unaware of the disaster that had happened outside of the church. Food, conversation, and drinks flowed freely to Cat's delight.

She spotted Ava and walked over to her surprised her sister hadn't gotten anything to eat yet. She was also surprised to see her alone. "Where's Folu?"

Cat vaguely listened as her sister made some lame excuse for her missing fiancé before Cat held out her plate to her. Ava declined and Cat felt her joy dampened a bit. Mini minefields still filled the elegant room. One wrong move and they'd detonate. Cat looked at Gwen dressed in a bright blood red gown (one of many she'd wear throughout the evening) as she spoke to Maya whose ankara dress almost appeared like a dingy housedress in comparison. Cat admired her sister's courage for showing up at the reception and said so.

"It wasn't her fault," Ava replied to Cat's off-handed comment about Maya.

Cat grinned. "Bet your eyes were closed when it happened."

"Only briefly."

"Right." Cat popped another delicious canapé in her mouth and absently listened to her sister defend Maya, not that it was necessary. Although Maya had rammed into Keeden with all the force of a linebacker it hadn't been intentional. But clearly the look on Gwen's face made it obvious she didn't think so. She would take no responsibility for what had happened. It was all Maya's fault. It was always Maya's fault.

"So what's the plan?" Cat asked Ava.

"Plan?"

"Yes. When are you going?"

Ava frowned. "I don't know what you mean."

It wasn't like her sister to be obtuse, there was definitely something different about her this evening, but Cat wouldn't press it. She tried to make her voice light. "No need to pretend you haven't been given orders."

Ava was the family ambassador. She would have to smooth things over between the families.

"Mom hasn't said anything yet," Ava said.

"She will."

But their father provided the summons instead. Cat watched Ava dutifully hurry over to the commandingly grim figure and nod at whatever he said.

She waited for their father to leave before she sneaked over to her sister and said, "So when are you going?"

Ava jumped, surprised by Cat's sudden appearance, before she said, "Soon."

"Want me to come with you?"

"I'd rather you go instead."

Cat's heart lifted. She needed her? This could be her chance to prove what she could do. Perhaps she could ruffle a few feathers in the process. "Really?"

"No, not really."

Cat's heart fell. "I would behave myself."

"Dad asked me. Besides, I have to leave before they cut the cake."

Cat's heart sunk further. "That's just mean. It's a chocolate raspberry cake with—"

"I don't care."

"I'll save a slice for you."

"Please don't."

She held out her plate again. "At least have something to eat before you go."

"I don't have an appetite."

Cat studied her for a moment. "Something's wrong."

"Nothing's wrong." Ava checked her watch. An object she didn't need but wore because it had been a gift from someone. That was Ava. Always thinking of someone else. "I might as well get going now."

Cat nodded sensing Ava wanted a reason to escape and knowing she had no way to figure out why.

Cat turned to see if she could talk to Maya but saw Maya effectively banished from the ballroom before Cat could reach her.

She sighed resigned and ate another canapé but this time it didn't taste nearly as good.

Later, she managed to smuggle a slice of wedding cake that she hoped to give to Maya since her sister hadn't had a chance to eat anything.

But a thief stole it during the night.

$$4$$

Cat happened upon the thief when she'd snuck into the kitchen around two in the morning to see if her contraband had been well hidden. She hadn't had a chance to give it to Maya yet because her sister remained locked away in her room and didn't reply to her knock, but she still hoped to give her the treat later in the day, only to discover it had been pilfered.

Her mother sat at the round kitchen table spitefully eating her bounty.

She'd unwrapped the carefully packaged slice without care and plopped it like gelatinous sludge onto a little pink saucer. The sweet confection now resembled the carcass of a dead creature the red raspberry filling reminding her of blood.

Cat gasped at the sight. "That was for Maya."

Her mother sent her an ugly look. "She doesn't deserve it," she said taking another large bite, her white teeth stained raspberry red.

The sight of her mother's action turned her stomach in two ways: one having to watch her mother eviscerating the cake with little care for how beautifully prepared it had been (Cat had wrapped it carefully so that Maya could see the design) or how delicious it was, and two that she'd set out to undermine Cat's efforts.

But she also sensed something darker, a true dislike for Maya that Cat could never understand and never wanted to. Her mother would have eaten an entire cake and made herself sick if it resulted in Maya not getting a single bite.

Cat sighed and let her shoulders fall in defeat.

Her mother sat back in triumph and tossed the fork against the saucer where it settled with a clatter.

"Clean this up," she said, slowly rising to her feet. "And don't ever try something like this again."

"I was just—"

Her mother's cutting glance stopped her words. Cat stared back at the beautiful face she hadn't inherited. The one with gorgeous brown skin, arresting brown eyes and a lovely mouth. The one complimented at every turn. But her mother's beauty hid a bramble choked heart that had scared Cat since she was a child. Her mother was a dark wilderness of spikes and bristles she'd had to carefully navigate by catering to, indulging and deflecting in order to keep peace in the house from her wrath.

Maya openly received the direct impact of this hidden monster, but Cat quietly had to see it and endure. She dutifully nodded at her mother's demand.

And the monster disappeared behind the beautiful mask once again. "Maya must know her place." She swept past her.

Days later Cat learned Maya would be sent before the firing squad—better known as a meeting with the elders.

The reason for this emergency meeting was due to a

second disaster Cat hadn't prepared for or predicted. She only found out about it when she overheard her mother on the phone profusely apologizing to someone.

She couldn't imagine what could be wrong. Everything was in order, wasn't it? She quickly went through a mental list.

Keeden would live.

Ava had smoothed the Kayodes relations with the Adesinas.

Gwen was off on her honeymoon.

Maya had sent flowers of apology.

Wait...Maya had sent flowers? The same Maya who hated flowers? The same Maya Cat had once seen gleefully cut petals off a rose with a pair of scissors?

How had that even happened? She must have been forced. So what had happened?

Cat stayed in her bedroom, going over the errands she had to run for the week, trying her best to stay out of the storm when her mother barged into the room (she never knocked, didn't feel the need to give anyone privacy, fortunately Cat could always hear her coming) and told her that she needed Cat to prepare food for a meeting with the elders.

That was never a good sign.

When she found out why (Maya had sent funeral flowers instead of a get-well-soon bouquet) Cat had inwardly laughed. Mystery solved. But it was all her mother's fault for forcing Maya to select flowers in the first place. Everyone knew how much her eldest sister hated them.

But because of that mistake Cat found herself with The List.

The List had come about when Cat was about twelve years old. She'd already lost the joys and freedom of childhood at about nine years old when her mother gave her the distinction of being her 'little helper' but really meant her 'little assistant' it sounded better than 'servant' but felt the same. Cat's duties included (but were not limited to) help polish shoes, clean the bathrooms, plus help catalog, coordinate and sort through what felt like endless stacks of cloth at the main shop. The only reprieve Cat was allowed were violin lessons because the son of one of her mother's rivals was getting lessons and her mother was not to be outdone.

Unfortunately, when Cat turned twelve her mother discovered Cat's true talent.

Tired of the drudgery of helping in the shop and with household chores, Cat innocently made the mistake of helping her mother with one of her hosted events by cooking some of the meals Cat had been practicing on her own in small batches.

The food received more praise than the event itself and at first Cat worried her mother would be upset.

Instead, her mother was delighted. And from that moment her mother stopped cooking. Instead she would hand Cat a list of events for any given month, along with a memo that explained the number of guests, who they were (naturally listed by level of importance) and a budget. With that Cat was expected to handle creating the menu, shopping for ingredients, cooking the meal and serving it (unless her mother wanted to hear praise and take the credit then she would serve the meal herself, which happened most times).

The only time Cat got a reprieve was if the guest list exceeded ten people then her mother would allow Cat to hire help, otherwise she'd say "This shows how much I trust you. What's there to complain about?" and not hear another word of protest.

So she didn't protest. Ever.

Instead, like now, Cat looked at The List and sighed. While Ava was the family diplomat, Cat's role was her mother's food patrol. Food was the Kayode family's weapon and shield. Every meal had to be strategic, created with a specific outcome in mind.

"Okay," Cat said, responding to the impatient tapping of her mother's shoe on the hard wood floor not softened by the purple area rug. "Give me a moment to look it over." She glanced over The List biting back a string of expletives.

Her duties included: making food for the elder meeting, cooking a pot of jollof rice to send to the Adesinas, cooking puff puffs for the pastor (why, her mother didn't say and Cat knew it was best not to ask) and then creating something for her mother's book club, which she was hosting that month. The food theme was to be Italian because the main character in the book they were reading had gone to an Italian villa.

When she asked which region in Italy the book was set, her mother just rolled her eyes and said it didn't matter. But to Cat food always mattered. Would she prepare something from Umbria or Tuscany or should it be Emilia Romagna or Sicilian?

"Anymore questions?" her mother said her impatience growing.

Cat shook her head and waited for her mother to leave before she fell back on her bed and swore.

Of course she had more questions. Lots more.

How could she make a meal that appeased the elders so that they were kinder to Maya than usual? What favor was her mother trying to get with the pastor? And why jollof rice for the Adesinas? Serving that side dish could be dangerous because Cat would have to decide which version to give— Nigerian? Ghanaian? (While Keeden's father and stepmother are Nigerian, his deceased mother had been from Ghana) Who should she cater to? The son or the parents? Should she try an Americanized or British version? Somewhere more neutral? Since she knew her mother had hastily made the request, Cat felt comfortable changing it without too much of a consequence.

She sat up and scratched out the jollof rice and left it blank. She'd later come up with a dish less controversial.

The budget was generous, but the time to complete these tasks less so. She'd have to stagger the various events, otherwise she'd get overwhelmed. She looked at her digital calendar and saw the elder meeting was the most pressing.

That afternoon, Ava treated her and Maya to lunch where they giggled over Maya's mistake and predicament and Cat had to hide what she knew was in store for her sister.

She left the luncheon armed with The List.

It was time to head to paradise.

5

———————

Paradise rose in all its lime green majesty at the far end of the shopping center. Its massive size dwarfed all the surrounding shops, while its arched entrance proclaimed its name, World Foods, in a haughty display.

Cat walked through the electric doors of the global market and welcomed the scent of grilled red peppers seasoned with a spice mix from India, one of the four food samples on display. The other spices hailed from Mexico, China and Egypt.

She made sure to avoid the tempting gentle allure of indulging in *just one taste*, knowing that if she stopped to taste one sample, she'd end up tasting them all and possibly buying all the spices as well and the items that paired best with them.

She had to focus.

She pushed her cart past a child being scolded in Spanish; down another aisle a child was being scolded in French, but the children's expressions were similar in their misery. She searched the frozen section while behind her a Caribbean couple, she couldn't quite place the accent, talked to the fishmonger; beside her an older couple argued in a Korean-English blend. Overhead the store announcer told customers about a sale on sumo oranges.

Sumo oranges? She loved those! She could make use of them in a...

No. No. She had to focus.

Cat was so determined not to be distracted by all the delights the market offered her that she almost didn't see him.

And not because he didn't stand out. Bryant Meadows always managed to stand out because he was tall, good looking with a charismatic air that was blinding.

He stood with his back to her, dressed in jeans and a long sleeve light orange shirt that complimented his dark skin, as he made his way through the Produce section.

She halted, gripping the handle of her full cart, calculating her options.

If he spotted her first he'd either look right through her and pretend he hadn't seen her or dart down an aisle and do his best to avoid her.

One thing, for sure, was he wouldn't be neutral. Cat could always get a rise out of him and this would be a surprise attack.

She glanced at her phone and saw the time. Her mother would expect her back soon. She could ignore him and finish her shopping or have a little fun.

She preferred fun.

Cat left her cart, making sure it was safely out of the way, then crept up behind Bryant where he'd stopped in front of a row of potatoes.

At first she wasn't sure what captured her attention more, the man or where he stood. His broad frame loomed tall in the center of a display of colors—vertical rows of yellow, red, and purple potatoes. There were also piles of jewel yams and Japanese sweet potatoes. The sight of them was so distracting she almost forgot her goal and forced herself to look at him again.

She watched as he carefully studied a boniato potato, and rubbed his thumb over it as if uncovering a rare gem. She could imagine him wondering how the sweet, chestnut like flavor could be used in soups or stews. Or was he considering a dessert? She stopped herself from asking and instead said, "Glad Keeden's okay."

He reacted as if she'd touched him with a live wire. His entire body jerked and he lost his grip on the potato. Cat watched it fly through the air and easily caught it before it fell on the ground.

She bit her lip, delighted by the effect she had on him. To everyone else she was overlooked and invisible but not him. Bryant kept his distance from her as much as he could and had an inherent dislike for her although it puzzled her as to why.

She held the potato out to him. "Have you spoken to him?"

Bryant pointedly ignored the offered object and chose another one. "I'm going to see him soon," he said in a stiff, distant voice.

The voice her sister Maya had probably never heard. Maya only saw Bryant as a beautiful man with a gorgeous smile. Her sister's crush was almost heartbreaking because Cat knew that the man her sister liked didn't really exist. If only she could whip out her phone and record him at moments like these when he wasn't friendly and charming and had the guarded gaze of a hunter not used to being prey.

Cat set the potato down on the pile. "That's good. Maya's meeting with the elders soon, not that I can warn her poor thing, but it's going to be bad so if you happen to see her be extra nice, okay?" She patted him on the back, feeling his muscles stiffen in protest to her touch. "Relax, it's a harmless request," she said then picked up the potato he'd been studying and placed it in his basket and added, "You've got good taste," before she began to turn.

But he stopped her by clearing his throat as if he wanted to say something. When she turned to him in question, his eyes met hers, which they hardly ever did, and she saw something unexpected. Something she'd never thought, never wanted, to see: A vulnerability.

Keeden's accident must have shaken him more than he'd care to admit if he was being this candid with her.

Bryant opened his mouth and Cat felt her heart kicking up speed with a mixture of anticipation and dread. She didn't want to have to console him, she wasn't good with emotions. And she felt he was the last person she should even try to.

But just as quickly as his expression had changed, it disappeared. He shifted his gaze from her face and stared at the plantain display as if it was somehow riveting and brusquely said, "See you," before he walked away.

Cat watched him go both puzzled and relieved. *What was that?* He wasn't supposed to act that way. He was supposed to scowl or grumble. Not look so...lost. She patted the front of her shirt, irritated by her unruly heart, and shook her head in dismay. That moment hadn't been fun at all.

But she also felt guilty for teasing him at such a time when she probably should have left him alone.

Cat sighed, grabbed some produce then took a picture and sent him a text.

It wasn't much and she doubted he'd even look at it but at least she'd tried and it made her feel better. Unknotting the tension that had settled within her by the passing look in his eyes.

Then she realized she'd been wrong, she had seen that look

before…years ago…a time she didn't want to remember anymore than he did.

But all thoughts of the past (and definitely Bryant) disappeared when Cat left the store, put her bags in the trunk of the car and headed a few shops down to her second favorite place.

There was nothing haughty or large about the wine and beer store, but it didn't have to be. Aisles of liquid pleasure whispered the promise of happy cocktail guests, wedding parties, fine dining, formal evenings or wild nights.

Cat entered the shop and nodded at the handsome, solemn faced man at the checkout register.

"Hey genius," she said.

She wasn't being facetious. The film school graduate had recently seen his New York dreams crash and burn, but still made small films on the side. Cat liked his work and felt confident with continued effort he'd grow his audience.

Her phone alerted her to a text. She glanced at it not surprised to see it was from him. *Working on another project.*

Looking forward to seeing it.

It'd be perfect for Halloween.

Oooh I like that.

Will send you some clips. Might give you ideas.

Or nightmares. She texted back knowing his movies tended to be weirdly, creepy and chillingly disturbing. The kind she liked.

<evil smile> You know it.

She looked over at him and he nodded once more in acknowledgement then gestured to the back where he knew she was headed.

She found her friend Vanessa Kapoor checking the shelves. She was one of the only friends Cat had managed to make as an adult. Vanessa and her family were transplants from Alabama and they'd bonded as a result of their mutual love of horror movies, immigrant parents with high expectations and music.

"Your brother is as talkative as ever," Cat said.

Vanessa saw her and grinned, giving her a big hug and Cat found herself briefly pressed against a full chest and engulfed in chubby, honey toned arms. Her friend stepped back and tucked a strand of dark hair behind her ear, the light catching its red highlights. "What are you doing here?"

"I don't have long," Cat said, always amazed that she could consider this vivacious, attractive woman a friend. Vanessa had many attributes that Cat lacked not only in looks but personality. She was never invisible. No one thought she had a sick sense of humor. And she had a bright future ahead of her because no one expected to keep her at home as their retirement plan.

"How was your sister's wedding?" she asked.

Cat groaned and from the expression on her face, Vanessa sensed a good story and told her brother to take care of things then led Cat to the back office where Cat tried to answer Vanessa's simple question as succinctly as possible but ended up losing twenty minutes, which she knew she'd pay for but didn't care. It was nice to have someone outside the family to commiserate with. Vanessa knew all about Cat's family dynamics.

"Are you ever going to tell your parents about us?"

Her parents thought Cat took evening and weekend cooking and accounting courses at the local college through an elective continuing education program. It was her only chance to carve out a life for herself. Instead, she and Vanessa practiced and performed as a musical duo at parties and events.

Not enough events to raise suspicions but enough to fill her life with fun.

"Probably not. They wouldn't understand."

She left the store with two of her mother's favorite wines and thought of drinking them all herself when Cat returned home and her mother casually informed her that the list of elders had gone from three to more, as if it was a minor inconvenience instead of a potential disaster. Fortunately, Cat had bought extra items in preparation for an unexpected change like that.

So she was more than prepared when the dreaded day arrived. Cat cooked early and swiftly. She wanted to get out of the house before the ambush (what her parents would deem an intervention) and there were certain disasters that gave her no pleasure. Because she knew who was coming she felt a little sorry for Maya. Her eldest sister would face a tough crowd, except for Uncle Martin.

In that instance, Cat felt a little sorry for him. He was their grandfather's surprise baby and was seven years younger than Maya and she never gave him the due respect he was expected to received (and desperately wanted) even though he tried.

Cat was only a little bit surprised when he was one of the first to arrive. She'd finish setting the food on the kitchen table when he walked into the room. He snuck a stuffed mushroom and she let him.

"Brave man," she said. "I didn't think you'd come."

For a moment he looked embarrassed then seemed to remember himself and his duty and straightened his shoulders. "It's expected."

"Maya will eat you alive."

He seemed to wilt a bit but then regained his courage.

"Maya's in a lot of trouble this time, and we've already come up with a solution."

The grin told her that whatever the solution was, it was going to make Maya miserable. "Are you going to tell me what it is?"

He shook his head. "I can't have you warning her."

She winced. "That bad, huh?"

He nodded and his grin grew.

"Don't look so smug. She won't go for it."

He popped another mushroom in his mouth before he spun on his heel to leave. "She won't have a choice."

6

———

EVERYTHING IS GOING to be OK.

Bryant frowned at the image of a grapefruit and two bananas spelling out the letters OK.

He rested his phone on the kitchen counter annoyed that he'd even looked at her message instead of deleting it.

He opened his bag and began to put his groceries away, trying not to think about Cat.

He wished he'd been prepared to turn and see that evil little grin of hers. He wasn't able to hide the affect she had on him.

And she loved it.

He put the lone boniato potato away, the one she'd handed back to him, even though he wanted to discard it because, dammit, it *was* good, and thought about what he'd cook it with tonight.

Everything is going to be OK.

It was a strange thing for her to text him, but perhaps she had a semblance of a heart after all.

But he didn't believe her. It was easy for her to say but he wasn't sure she meant it.

Sure, the greatest crisis, Keeden being hit by a car, was over now and his friend was healing nicely, but there was still so many other worries that occupied his mind.

The renovations on his house would soon start. Fortunately, he'd be staying at Keeden's house during the time because he worked from home and would find the noise too distracting, but part of him still wondered if the renovation was a good idea. How his father would react. He worried about his father a lot even though he lived happily in an assisted living facility and came to visit and stay once a month. He hadn't consulted him about any of the changes.

Everything is going to be OK.

And aside from his father Bryant was worried about Keeden. They had a successful design and graphic business that licensed their work, and they also collaborated on illustrated books.

But before the accident Keeden had been struggling with a woodblock commission. This accident hampered that process, but if he got some help...and perhaps some rest and a new perspective of the project might be what he needed.

Everything is going to be OK.

Then there was the project with his mother that had come unexpectedly but was dear to his heart. But they still had their differences...

Everything is going to be OK.

Cat had become an unwanted pattern. She always seemed to come into his life when he was at a crossroads.

Or something major was about to change, when he felt his world would come to an end.

Which reluctantly reminded him of when he'd first met her.

7

———

TWENTY YEARS AGO…

"YOU'RE NOT GOING TO DIE."

Bryant looked out the one eye that hadn't been swollen shut by the blows of his attackers; pushing through a pain soaked haze he tried to see the source of the voice.

And saw the ugliest little angel.

Not that he believed in angels. But for some reason that's the first thought that came to mind: A cosmic joke that the end of his seventeen years on earth would be with this strange looking creature while he lay on the hot Georgia grass.

His angel was a child—seven, eight, maybe nine—with a child's high pitched voice, like the upper register on a flute, but that's all that matched. The rest of the angel formed a body that seemed to be a strange mixture of shapes. Small eyes, like shiny dark marbles, set in a brown, round face. The rest of the creature reminded him of a toy made up of rectangular blocks: Long and thin torso, long neck, and long arms.

"You're going to be okay."

The ugly angel said the words so calmly he believed her.

Breathing hurt. Everything hurt. And yet he still believed her. Felt comforted by her.

But why was he thinking about something he didn't even believe in?

She turned quickly as if alerted to something he couldn't hear or sense then said, "I'll be right back," before she left him. And he felt bereft wishing he had the strength to grab her and force her to stay because he didn't want to be alone.

Then he remembered he hadn't been alone. His heart began to pound harder to the beat of doom. Before the attack he'd been with his father. Where was his Dad? Every part of his body screamed in protest as he tried to lift himself to a sitting position.

"No, don't move yet," the ugly angel said, returning to his side, sliding thin, nimble fingers through his, clasping her hand with his.

He moved his mouth but no words came out. He had to tell her about his father.

"He's okay," she said quickly, understanding his concern. "You're both going to be okay." She began to hum a song he knew but couldn't place. A classical tune that strangely filled his mind with the image of dancing fairies and castles. And castles made him think of clouds and soon he was floating high above the pain that kept him grounded to the new land he still hadn't managed to understand even after four years. He flew high above the taunts and jeers about the British accent he hadn't managed to completely eradicate, the poor marks he received from teachers, the disappointment his mother hadn't managed to hide in her gaze.

He floated on the song being hummed by the ugly little angel and he didn't want to come back down.

And perhaps he wouldn't have if the ambulance's piercing siren hadn't drowned out her voice.

Unwanted tears began to fall and it hurt to cry but he couldn't seem to stop himself. As the terror of what had happened rushed forward in his mind, his sense of helplessness, his humiliation, his fear.

He felt her hand on his forehead.

"You're not going to die," the ugly angel said again then she was gone.

A whirl of activity, he could barely remember later, swept through the edges of his memory over the next few days. He slipped in and out of consciousness. Heard questions he couldn't answer, voices he couldn't distinguish, saw unfamiliar faces, and sights that mingled with rough hands and pungent smells.

Then he woke up, clearheaded at last, to the sound of rain against the window, the smell of cigarettes coming off a coat left on the back of a chair next to another bed. It took him a moment to realize he was in a hospital.

A rosy faced nurse, a man with biceps the size of footballs, came over to him and said something in a Southern Georgia drawl that Bryant was still getting used to and couldn't quite decipher.

Georgia wasn't like Texas or Arizona where they'd briefly lived when they'd first arrived in the States for his mother's medical studies. Bryant wasn't even sure if Arizona was considered the south. He'd gotten in trouble for mixing the different regions before.

"I'm sorry?" Bryant said because the man kept talking and Bryant didn't know what he was saying.

"I said, you're a lucky one," the man repeated without annoyance, his voice bright and cheerful. Bryant found it weird that someone could sound like an amusement park mascot in a place filled with sickness and pain.

Lucky? The man thought he was lucky? Bryant didn't feel lucky; hadn't felt so in years, but he was too tired to argue.

"Don't get me wrong," the nurse said, "but with a beating like yours, you're lucky it wasn't worst. They'd only broken bones."

The nurse went on to explain that Byrant had been fortunate to escape with his brain intact—no cerebral hemorrhage—and nothing busted inside—no internal bleeding.

Which sounded callous but Bryant knew the nurse was trying to comfort him, although the man had the bedside manner of a gangster. Soon the nurse was chatting about busted spleens, collapsed lungs, exploding hearts and other horrors that could result from a massive beating. He cheerfully congratulated Bryant on getting away with just the 'clean breaks': Two broken ribs, a busted shoulder, and ankle. They hadn't shattered his jaw. Yes, he'd been lucky there too, although an X-ray had spotted a tiny fracture on the back of his skull that would quickly heal because he was young.

Before the nurse left, Bryant managed to say, "My fa—"

"He's lucky too," the nurse said with a big grin, saving Bryant the energy of finishing his sentence. "I heard you two were very fortunate that kid was around."

"Kid?"

The man chuckled. "Fooled us all. Demanded to ride in

the ambulance with your father saying she was his daughter and then disappeared. But from what I've heard she was the one who'd called. Witnesses even said she was the one who'd stopped the attack."

"Who is she?"

"We thought you'd know. Never heard of a kid so brave. Those bastards could have done a number on her if she hadn't scared them off with a whistle and shouting 'Fire' or somethin'."

She wasn't real. That's why no one could find her. She had been an angel. An ugly little angel had saved his life and he'd never forget it. Or her.

HE SPENT NEARLY two weeks in the hospital, recovering from an infection after one of his surgeries, but managed to return home with his mind focused on only one thing.

Her.

His angel.

The first chance Bryant got, he tried to draw what he'd remembered of her.

But it took a month to realize his life had changed in a way his angel couldn't save him from. While his father had left with seemingly minor injuries compared to his, they soon learned that the damage to his brain had been more extensive than first thought.

As a result of the beating, his father suffered memory and cognitive issues that caused him to lose his job and eventually ended his marriage to a woman who had no use for a man who wasn't the confident professional she'd met.

Bryant had no problem leaving Georgia with his father to

move to New York where they stayed with a cousin. Bryant was able to finish his studies while also looking after his dad.

And he kept a picture of the angel with him. Every year he'd draw another rendition of her.

"What a strange face," an aunt once said when she'd caught him drawing in the corner of the cramped apartment living room.

Bryant only grunted. He didn't care what anyone else thought of her face, that wasn't what he was trying to capture. It was the strange sense of knowingness, of certainty. He'd been terrified only moments before. He'd thought he'd die. He remembered the dread that had slithered over his skin when the group of guys surrounded him and his father when they were one block away from his high school. His father had taken the bus to meet him and planned to treat them both to milkshakes at a diner a few blocks away.

He remembered the rage in their eyes. Bryant remembered searching his mind for a solution, desperately wondering how he and his father could get away from them without injury. Frantically trying to figure out why they'd targeted them in the first place. He hadn't said anything to them, hadn't looked at them; didn't even know them, except in passing. In school, he kept his head down, focused on his studies and his art and that was all.

He didn't like causing trouble; he didn't like being afraid.

But trouble had found him.

His father tried to placate them, but they were out for blood. All because of what he'd decided to wear that day.

It was only later that Bryant realized his mistake: That the boys had confused the bright white cross on his red, white and blue Union Jack T-shirt with the Confederate flag.

They were going to 'teach them a little history lesson.'

That's what one of the attackers sneered before his fist, which felt like it had been dipped in cement, knocked Bryant to the ground.

It still enraged him that the Georgia boys' inability to distinguish the British flag from the Confederate flag had cost Bryant so much. His parents' marriage, the confident, successful father he'd loved and a sense of security.

After that attack he became a man afraid.

But before that, for a moment—the barest, sweetest of moments—he hadn't been scared because of his angel.

He hadn't feared death, pain, loss, even though every breath hurt, he was glad to be alive. Because of those strange marble eyes and high pitched voice of a child that held the wisdom of ages.

And there was the humming. A song he knew but couldn't place until later: Tchaikovsky's *Dance of the Sugar Plum Fairies* and Puccini's *O mio babbino caro*.

Why had a kid been humming those classical songs? But of course it was because she wasn't real. An angel didn't do ordinary things. At times Bryant wondered if he could conjure her up again. He wondered if she was looking over him without his knowing. It gave him comfort to think so.

His life had been about loss.

His mother hadn't come to visit him in New York as she'd promised she would. She could never find the time. He'd been bitterly disappointed until he realized listening to her excuses over the phone were the only times he'd hear her voice.

Soon the broken promises didn't matter anymore and he stopped expecting anything more.

Because he had his angel. Someone who truly looked out for him and he sensed, an indescribable sense of anticipation and longing, that he'd see her again.

That is was fated.

He believed in fate even less than he did in angels but the idea wouldn't leave his mind. The attack had changed him.

His best friend Keeden, the first true friend he'd allowed himself to make after the incident, teased him that Bryant's angel had become an obsession and he didn't deny it.

Anytime he felt anxious about something; couldn't figure out something, he found himself drawing the ugly angel and feeling calm again.

But he never imagined that place of sanctuary wouldn't last.

$$8$$

Eᴵɢʜᴛ ʏᴇᴀʀs ʟᴀᴛᴇʀ…

Iғ sʜᴇ ʜᴀᴅɴ'ᴛ sᴘᴏᴋᴇɴ he never would have recognized her.

Bryant stood on the balcony of the New Jersey mansion for the third time wondering how he'd allowed Keeden to bribe him to attend the party with him. Keeden had stronger ties to the Nigerian-American community than Bryant did, being only half-Nigerian on his mother's side.

Keeden's family—namely his father—had expected his son to show himself at the celebration of a family friend's second daughter completing her residency at a prestigious hospital.

As two MFA graduates with part-time jobs, freelance work to fill in the gaps and a struggling graphic design company, he and Bryant were merely tolerated and quickly ignored. This was how Bryant found himself alone on the balcony, picking his way through the various offerings on his plate, while a light breeze skimmed across the surface of the large swimming pool below, creating a ripple of tiny waves.

That's how his life felt, like a ripple of waves that were slowly increasing. He wondered how they could drum up more business.

Or if they'd made a giant mistake trying to make it on their own.

He picked up one of the fried spinach pancakes the host had piled on his plate and took a bite. He managed to hold back a grimace since it tasted like salted paper. He looked with horror that she'd given him three. He'd at least finish one to be polite.

"You only have to pretend to like it," a voice said behind him, "you don't have to eat it too."

Bryant turned and pasted on a smile, because that was his habit, but his lips froze in place at who or rather what stood in front of him: an extraordinarily plain faced teenager with a strange voice of authority.

His mind grew blank for a moment and he found that he didn't know what she was talking about. Or who she was. Clearly she was from one of the prominent families that Keeden's father wanted to impress, from her expensive black shift dress—which oddly made her appear as if she were attending a funeral, instead of a more festive gathering—and haughty manner (only someone who came from money could look that plain and yet be condescending).

She wore leaf-shaped gold earrings and had a short bob that did little to improve her looks, which remained as unre-markable as driftwood. He thought perhaps she'd confused him for someone else because there was a familiar way that she looked at him, addressed him, stood near him that he found both thrilling and unsettling.

"I'm sorry?"

"Those nasty spinach cakes, you don't have to eat them."

She lowered her voice then glanced around before she said, "I can make them disappear for you if you want," but before allowing him to reply, she took a napkin, covered his plate and grabbed the offending pancakes before making them disappear into her handbag. "You're welcome."

He stared at her speechless, wondering why such a weird little thing wanted to talk to him.

"You can stop smiling now. You're a good looking guy but that smile's a little creepy."

His smile fell. No one had ever said that to him before. And the only creepy thing around was *her*. But he took a deep breath, reminding himself not to be annoyed. He was an adult and she a child. He'd remain mature no matter what careless remarks she said.

She surveyed his plate. "You should be safe now." She pointed to the water biscuits topped with prawns and chopped mangoes and mint. "These are delicious. I..." She paused, cleared her throat, "I mean my mother made them so I'm a little biased but trust me. They're good. The fresh lime juice squeezed over them makes all the difference."

He hesitated then took a bite, feeling the intensity of her gaze. He was about to quickly swallow then stopped and let the flavors tantalize all his senses. It wasn't good. It was delicious. Heaven. He ate another one.

She folded her arms, satisfied.

"I knew you wouldn't die."

He frowned. That was a strange statement to make. "I don't think any of the dishes are bad enough to kill."

She shook her head. "I'm not talking about the food. I'm talking about before."

Bryant blinked. Before? Had they met before? The unsettling feeling began to grow.

Then he saw her smile.

Instead of a pen he would have used the edge of a spatula to draw it. It was that harsh, a little cold.

He felt a chill grip him.

And in seconds he was back in Georgia, flat on his back, a frightened teenager riddled with pain, crying.

And an ugly little angel had...

But no here she was. All grown up. Well, partially grown. That had to be wrong. Angels didn't grow up, did they?

His mouth suddenly went dry. His throat closed. She wasn't supposed to be real. Irrationally he felt betrayed, shattered, left drifting again as if his world had been destroyed once more.

His angel, his ugly angel had never existed. It had all been a delusion.

Bryant didn't want to admit that she'd been an ordinary kid. Okay, a kid who'd done an extraordinary thing, but ordinary all the same. Not magical, not amazing. Not safe.

She'd seen him at his worse. She'd seen him cry. He'd felt safe with her and now realized he hadn't really been. He'd been vulnerable and weak. Would she remember that too? Not just recognize him, but recognize his fears?

Was that the meaning of that cold, haughty smile?

He'd always feel exposed by her because she knew too much. He couldn't pretend with her. Those beady little eyes hadn't changed. He could fool everyone else but not her. Never her. That scared him.

He hated being scared.

He'd designed his life to keep himself safe. He had casual relationships with women who learned not to expect too much from him and he expected even less from them (aside from one mistake he still regretted). He had a best friend, the only person (aside from his father) that he allowed close, and many acquaintances he didn't. But they'd never know it. He let them think they were close because it was easier that way.

His closest relationship was with his art.

She hadn't told anyone else about their meeting. If she had he was sure people would have mentioned it but they never did and he was glad.

He wondered how she'd ended up alone that day long ago in Georgia; what story she'd told her parents when she returned home.

But he didn't like wondering about her. He didn't like thinking of her having parents and siblings and being so ordinary and ripping away the talisman she'd once been to him.

It wasn't her fault but he hated her a little for it. For not only being ordinary but also being so very plain.

He'd tried to capture her in his memory but it had been so far from the truth. Of course age had made the rectangles appear harsher, the eyes smaller, the roundness of youth giving way to an angular arrogance.

He'd never trust this woman.

She scared him too much.

She reminded him that he hadn't been able to save his father from a foolish choice he'd made. Wearing the T-shirt had been his idea and if his father hadn't come to pick him up that day...

"How's your dad?"

Bryant gripped his hand into a fist. Was that a joke? His past always seemed to follow him at gatherings like this. Everyone seemed to know what had driven him and his father from Georgia. Since his parents' divorce people spoke about his father in whispers.

The black British son of a lorry driver who'd managed to

marry up (his wife had gone to uni; he hadn't) and worked hard to get a managerial position at a medical clinic. Until the incident where people delicately mentioned his father's debilitating panic attacks and inability to keep a job for long and the son he depended on and how it must have been so difficult for his wife to break from a man who would have curtailed her ambitions.

Nobody truly asked about his father without the tinge of polite insincerity or out of an absurd curiosity. At times Bryant wanted to respond to their inane questions with, "He started crying for half an hour and I couldn't console him" or "He's lamenting how much I'd be better off without him again." But he didn't say any of that because he was too well-mannered and wanted to keep those hard moments to himself, instead he said, "He's fine," in a curt tone that usually ended things.

But the plain faced teenager narrowed her beady, dark eyes and rested her hands on her hips, studying him. "Why do you pretend so much?"

He held her gaze and said in a dark tone of menace. One he only used when he felt threaten. "I'm not pretending."

She shrugged, clearly not believing him and that incensed him more. But she didn't seem to sense his animosity when she returned her gaze to his plate again. "You know you really should try—"

"Cat," someone called to her, "you're needed."

Cat? This creature didn't look like a cat. Even a rat would have been too elegant a comparison. She reminded him of an insect. Bryant shifted his gaze to the attractive older woman standing in the doorway. She smiled at him as if in regret that he was being bothered.

The teenager gestured to Bryant with one of her long fingers. "Mom, I was just—"

Mom?

"This is not a discussion," the woman said, effectively snipping her daughter's words while still sounding pleasant. Cat's mother nodded at Bryant. "Excuse us," she said before she turned and left, her words reminding him of an apology as if her daughter was an embarrassment to her. He could understand why.

He stared, amazed that the plain faced teenager would come from such a striking woman. And yet there was something about the older woman that made him happy to see her go.

Cat sighed, waved a feeble goodbye and quietly followed behind.

~

"You DEFINITELY GOT THE EYES RIGHT," Keeden said as he and Bryant weaved their way through the row of cars to get to the rental that would drive them back to their lives in DC.

"What?"

"That's her, right? That girl who talked to you on the balcony. She's your angel."

Bryant gritted his teeth. "No, she isn't."

Keeden knew he was lying and Bryant hoped his friend would follow along, but he didn't. "Then there's a remarkable likeness."

"It's not her."

"I saw you two talking and there was this moment where a look came over your face—"

"It's not her."

"As if you'd seen a ghost," Keeden finished.

Bryant swore. "I don't know what you saw. Or think you saw. But it's nothing."

"She—"

"It's not her."

Keeden held out his hand. "Let me see."

"What?"

"Your phone. The angel is still your screensaver, right?"

It would be the first thing he'd delete. He glared at his friend. Keeden stared back unfazed. Although Keeden didn't reach Bryant's height or his size, he was not tall and on the slender side, he could still make Bryant feel small.

Bryant swore and reluctantly handed the phone to him. Keeden took it and nodded. "She's sort of beautifully plain, you know?"

He snatched the phone and shoved it back inside his jacket pocket. "No, I don't know."

"What did you say to her?"

"Nothing."

Keeden's brows shot up. "Not thanks for saving my life?"

"She seemed pleased enough with herself," Bryant said in a sour tone. "She didn't need me to congratulate her."

Keeden frowned. "That's not the impression I got. I'm surprised she's never told anyone about your connection. The way rumors spread in our community, if she had, you would have known about it. Seems she's discreet and not one to brag. That's admirable."

Bryant didn't want to give her the benefit. She'd called him a pretender (damn her she was right) and then told him he had a creepy smile. His smile was his greatest asset.

His angel had truly died. And the loss hurt. "Doesn't matter. I hope never to see her again."

When Bryant returned home, he considered burning all

his sketches of her. He imagined doing it, he even planned it. Every action, every motion, every detail, but when the chance came he froze. Every single time.

Once, he even tore one of his sketches of her in half and felt so miserable afterwards the only way he'd managed to feel better was to re-sketch it.

He couldn't get rid of her. But he could stay away. He did so the best he could.

From those knowing, judging eyes.

But then came Arizona.

AN ALERT on his phone stopped Bryant from being sucked into the power of that stinging memory and pulled him fully into his present life in Maryland.

He looked at the alert and frowned.

His father had sent nearly four hundred dollars to someone Bryant had never heard of.

9

___

The violets were drooping.

Bryant made a note to himself to water the plant before he left. His father liked to have flowers around him but didn't always remember to tend to them. It had been a job of his father's second wife: A caterer who'd arrived from Grenada, twenty-five years ago and seen past his father's failings to the gentle, kind man beneath.

Meredith's presence in his father's life had been a welcome addition and had allowed Bryant to not have to worry about his father as much. It had allowed Bryant to travel and eventually settle in Maryland while his father continued his life in New York. He called and visited frequently taking pleasure in how happy his father was.

And perhaps that would have lasted for another twenty or thirty years—they were a great match and the marriage was solid until, three years ago; the day Meredith arrived at the hospital experiencing nausea and extreme fatigue. The doctors misdiagnosed her heart attack as an anxiety attack and gave her medicine for it before unwittingly sending her home to die.

After addressing the shock that impacted both their lives, Bryant made arrangements for his father to move into an assisted-living facility close to him in Maryland. He wanted to give his father independence but one thing he continued to monitor was his expenses.

Bryant sat at the small dining table in his father's one bedroom apartment and sipped the black tea—too much milk and not enough sugar—his father had poured wondering how best to broach the subject. He nibbled on one of his Dad's favorite shortbread cookies and studied the grey haired man whose starched, white shirt was so bright it could likely glow in the dark. His father only wore long sleeved, button down shirts. He said it felt like a privilege since the shirts reminded him of the office workers he'd admired as a youth rather than the worn T-shirts of the laborers he'd grown up with.

Bryant heard a light tapping against the window and turned and saw a bee hitting the glass. It was clearly more interested in the wilted flower sitting on the ledge than the flowers in the landscaped garden gracing the courtyard below.

Bryant set the half eaten shortbread down and decided to get to the point.

"Dad, who's Gareth?"

His father smiled. "Oh, he's a very nice young man who helps out at the rec center."

The bee continued to tap against the window. *Buzz, tap, buzz, tap.* Bryant tried to ignore it. "And why did you send him money?"

His smile faded and his soft brown eyes grew sad. "Well, it's a very sad story…"

Bryant silently swore. Of course that's how it would begin. His father was a sucker for a sob story and fell for most of them.

"He's had to drop out of school to take care of his sick—"

"Mother?" Bryant guessed.

"No, his grandmother."

Buzz, tap, buzz, tap. "Right, of course."

His father continued, not picking up on Bryant's sarcasm.

"She's the one who raised him when—"

"His parents died."

"No, only his father died. His mother's in prison for fraud."

"I see," Bryant said impressed. This kid told a great story. No wonder his father fell for it.

Buzz, tap, buzz, tap. Bryant walked over to the window and moved the violets from view. "So what did he need the money for?"

"The electricity bill was about to be cut off and his grandmother needs her medicines to stay cool in a special fridge. She used to be married to a successful businessman, he said his grandfather had been well-respected, but when he died she was left vulnerable and her second husband, went through most of her savings and left her with only a small income to live on. Poor woman."

"Okay..." Bryant said returning to his seat, "and he just told you all this out of the blue?"

"No, I had to get it out of him. I caught him swiping some food at the center and you know people like talking to me."

People like *taking* from you, Bryant wanted to say, but didn't.

"...so I thought I'd help him out," his father was saying.

Buzz, buzz, tap, tap. Bryant glared at determined little insect hitting the window. What was wrong with this bee? He took a deep breath and looked at his father again. "I'd like to meet this Gareth."

His father's smile widened with delight. "I'd like you to meet him too. He's a fine young man."

"Yes, but in the meantime we have to come to an agreement that you don't spend more than a hundred without telling me."

His father frowned. "I've been managing my money—"

"I know, but we agreed about creating the 'generous fund' after what happened, remember?"

The 'generous fund' was the name for money his father was free to spend. His father still had his own account and on more than one occasion had befriended people who always found themselves in financial need.

Bryant knew he was luckier than most when it came to his father's finances. His father trusted him and let him handle all the money, a habit he'd had to gain from necessity after the accident and his father kept making mistakes. The budgeting had been a task his step-mother used to do. Meredith had managed to keep him in line but after her passing (which had left him with a comfortable inheritance), and no one to gently protect or correct him, his father had gone back to his old ways. So Bryant tried to keep a close eye but hadn't thought much about it.

Until Mary Wilkins, a clever, fast-talking interior designer in her fifties. She had convinced his father they were in love and bilked him out of nearly ten thousand before Bryant caught on. His father had been embarrassed but had finally revealed the truth. He told him about how they were truly in love and that they were building a business together where Mary was using her design skills to show seniors and low income individuals how to design on a budget. They had a website and she'd told him she'd gotten investments from local furniture businesses and she was working on generating more funding.

Naturally, it didn't take much digging to discover there was no business.

Mary conveniently disappeared too.

His father's broken heart angered Bryant more than the loss of the money.

"That was just once," his father said, sounding like a sulky child. He sipped his tea then carefully set it down. "She seemed like such a nice woman."

Bryant slowly counted to ten. "I know, but we know that many people only act nice because they want something from you."

His father frowned. "That's a very cynical thing to say."

Cynical yes, but true. "And I mean it. We don't want it to happen again." Bryant sighed, he didn't like to make his father unhappy or think that he wasn't treating him with respect. "I'm not saying you can't help people, just let me know when it's over a certain amount. Okay?"

He nodded. "Don't worry. He's a good young man. You'll like him."

Bryant bit into another shortbread cookie to hide his frown.

10

———

The house felt empty without Maya.

The elders had decided that Maya's punishment would be to live and work with Keeden and help him with his project: Maya's worst nightmare.

Cat was certain her sister would protest. That she'd come up with a clever scheme to get out of it. There was no way Maya could be forced to work with a man she hated.

But then Bryant Meadows ruined everything.

Cat stood at the stove and scooped up a spatula full of crisp yams and set them on a plate, trying not to remember the unease she'd felt at dinner the other night when Maya dreamily told Cat and Ava why she'd work with Keeden.

Because of Bryant.

Bryant was also staying there while he had renovations done on his house and she hoped to increase her chances with him.

Her sister's crush on Bryant worried her.

Ava was equally worried but for different reasons. She could spot a pretender because she was a master at the game.

But Cat knew Bryant better than either her sisters did, however she'd never tell them. Details of his past were not for her to share. And she didn't want anyone to know how she'd first met him. The reasons she'd been alone that day. What she'd been up to.

"Don't let the butter burn," her mother said coming into the kitchen.

"I'm not using butter," Cat said softly, suddenly aware of how the heat in the kitchen clung to her skin, how the edges of the sliced yams sizzled. "It's oil."

"Don't let the oil burn."

She'd never done that. It was a mistake her mother tended to make, but giving Cat instructions made her mother feel important.

Her mother speared one of the fried yams and ate it, humming a happy tune to herself.

The tune meant her mother was pleased. She'd never admit it but her mother was in a good mood now that Maya was gone.

Her mother had the same pleased expression when Maya had been forced to leave at nineteen.

Cat hated her a little for that. She didn't know why her mother had such strong feelings against Maya. But for Cat it had been a loss. Maya hadn't only been a caring sister, she'd been like the mother their own mother couldn't be. She made her feel loved and worthy.

On rare occasions she'd look at her mother and catch a glimpse of a woman afraid. Of what, Cat could never figure out. Her mother's façade was too carefully honed and crafted to allow such a revelation.

But her joy was no façade. Her mother had gotten exactly what she'd wanted: Maya out of the house.

Cat still didn't let her guard down. Her mother's moods were changeable and Maya could still make a mistake that affected them all.

She'd learned that anything was possible.

11

————

BRYANT MADE his way through the large rec center, greeted with the smell of chlorine from the indoor swimming pool, loud squeak of shoes and the pounding of a ball hitting the hardwood floor in the basketball court.

He walked into the large multipurpose room where he spotted the only person under the age of fifty, helping put away some chairs. A board to the side provided a clue of the event that had just finished. 'A Guide to Estate Planning' with a picture of a man in a grey suit with paper white teeth and hair dyed blacker than crude oil. In person the man looked the same, except the suit was now a dark green, and surrounded by people eager to take his card. Fortunately, his father wasn't one of them. But Bryant wasn't there for that.

He was a scruffy looking light skinned guy, who looked like he could use a good shower and shampoo. His jeans and shirt looked as if he'd stolen them from a jumble sale.

Bryant wondered if the kid really worked at the center or had gone there unnoticed and pretended to be one of the staff.

His father spotted Bryant and waved him over and eagerly said, "I just listened to an amazing speech."

"Not now Dad," Bryant said gently. "Where's Gareth?" he asked even though he knew exactly where he was.

His father glanced around then paused when his gaze fell on the young man. "Gareth!" his father called out to him and at first the man turned and smiled but his lips froze in place when he saw Bryant. Fear lit his eyes.

Bryant smiled back. *Yes, that's right. You'd better be worried.* They walked over to him.

"This is my son, Bryant," his father said, not noticing how tense the young man had become. "I've been telling him so much about you."

Gareth dipped his head embarrassed. "There's not much to tell."

"Oh, there was plenty," Bryant said. "Will you be on your break soon?"

Gareth looked around and began to say, "Uh...I'm..." before he realized it wasn't a question. His shoulders drooped. "Yeah."

"I'll meet you back at the apartment," he said to his father then to Gareth he said, "Follow me."

They walked to the hallway where he overheard Gareth say, "I knew it was too good to be true."

Bryant spun to him. "Because you thought he'd be an easy target?"

"No, no," Gareth said quickly. "B-because it came just in time. I was so relieved." He held up his hands. "Look, I didn't ask. I know I shouldn't have been on the phone when I should have been working but I had to do something or my gran would be in trouble. And I didn't spend it all. I can give you some of it back and work off the rest."

"You're a hard worker?"

"Yes, sir."

"Does your grandmother know you work here?"

There was the briefest hesitation before he said, "I don't work here, I volunteer."

"You have time to volunteer?"

His gaze slid away. "Yeah."

Bryant still couldn't read him. Up close he appeared older than he'd first seemed, possibly in his mid-twenties. And although he looked scruffy, he smelled like cheap soap and was clean shaven. He was clever. Either he volunteered for the access to food or targets.

Bryant folded his arms. "My dad's talked so much about your grandmother I'd like a chance to meet her."

For a moment Gareth looked panicked and Bryant's suspicions grew. "She doesn't like visitors."

"It'll be a quick visit," Bryant said, "I think she'd like to know what a great kid she's raised."

He rubbed his hands against his jeans. "You really don't have to do that."

"Here's the deal. I meet your grandmother and consider it equal. You get to keep the money and nothing has to be paid back. Or I work you until the entire amount is paid. What will it be?"

Gareth glared at him. It was a worthy effort that left Bryant amused rather than touched. He rested his hands on his hips and held the boy's gaze with a look he saved for business associates who tried to underestimate him.

Gareth blinked rapidly then let his gaze fall. "I'll work for you."

Of course he would. "You saw an easy target, didn't you?" Bryant sneered, glad he'd uncovered the young man's true intentions. "A simple man, with simple tastes and a good heart and you thought, Why not? He's living here so he's got money and he wouldn't miss it. He's a daft—"

Eyes lit with fire met his and for a moment Bryant was shaken. The young man released a litany of rapid-fast Spanish that Bryant didn't think he'd manage to understand even if he did speak the language.

Once Gareth had finished his string of insults (Bryant couldn't imagine them being anything else), Bryant rested his hands on his hips and said, "Care to translate? Or do you want me to guess?"

A touch of regret reddened his face. "I don't like you talking about him like that. Mr. Meadows is the finest man I know," Gareth said his voice shaking with restrained anger, "and I'd never hurt him. I—" his words abruptly broke off and he swore. Bryant turned and saw what had caught the young man's attention: an older black man with a distinguished mustache, dressed in a green blazer had his hand wrapped around the waist of a giggling older woman wearing an outfit that made it clear she was ready for a night on the town.

"You know him?" Bryant asked.

Gareth gave a curt nod. "Grandmother's boyfriend."

Bryant turned quickly back to the man before he and his companion disappeared around the corner. Suddenly, the pieces began to fit. "Is he the reason you're here?"

"I knew he wasn't to be trusted, but my grandmother wouldn't listen. You think she would have learned after... anyway so I did a little digging and followed him here and I've been watching him."

Bryant saw a younger version of himself. He knew that look, that feeling of worry when you're helpless to protect someone you care about.

"How much has she given him?"

Gareth's gaze fell.

"I'm guessing four hundred dollars?"

His head snapped up in surprise. "Yeah. She told me he said he'd pay it back, but... I have a night job and come here when I can."

Which meant he barely got any sleep; no wonder he looked so disheveled.

This time Bryant was the one to look away as shame broke through his arrogance. He'd been quick to judge, by filling in gaps with his own prejudice.

When had he become so cynical and suspicious? When had he stopped seeing his father as a great man? He'd been up too close for too long. It was as if he'd been looking at the imperfect brushstrokes of a painting instead of taking a step back and seeing a masterpiece.

Bryant now saw himself in this young man's gaze and didn't like what he saw. He'd grown hard because he'd had to for his father's sake (and for his own survival), but he'd also let his heart grow hard. Relationships had come and gone with little notice or care because he didn't let anyone close. Didn't care to really trust anyone.

Bryant sighed. "I'm sorry."

Gareth gave a stiff nod before he said in a tight voice, "I look out for him."

"I know. Thanks."

"I'll give—"

Bryant waved his words away. "No, you don't have to do that."

"But I don't want you to think—"

"I don't."

Bryant felt his pulse pick up pace even before he let the

idea settle in his thoughts. The young man had skills he might be able to use. He'd managed to track his grandmother's boyfriend and follow him undetected.

He had a lot to worry about with all the renovations going on at his place.

"I could use someone like you."

Gareth narrowed his eyes. "Doing what?"

"Exactly what you're doing now. Looking out for my dad just as you're doing for your grandmother. I'll pay you to report back to me if you see anything out of the ordinary."

Gareth shifted from one foot to the other, uneasy. "He's my friend. I don't like spying."

"That's fine. I won't force you." He turned, waited a few beats.

"But...if it'd help."

He slowly turned back. "It would."

Gareth rubbed his chin. "My shift starts at—"

"You're not working that job anymore. I'm hiring you for the year, maybe longer. I'll draw up a contract and everything so you and your grandmother can look it over." He grinned. "I'm sure you've already looked me up and know that I can afford it. "You'll be an assistant. No one needs to know the truth."

"Okay," Gareth said and to Bryant's annoyance the word reminded him of the image of a pineapple and two bananas spelling out the letters.

12

He felt as if he was being unfaithful. With his worries about his father settled, the renovations on his house underway and Keeden beginning to work on his commission again, Bryant focused on his second love: Food.

But as Bryant sat on Keeden's patio and enjoyed another chef-created dinner with Maya (Keeden still refused to join them), while the spring day welcomed the coming evening in a warm, orange haze, all he could think about was Mrs. Kayode's fluffy, rich coconut rice and spicy egusi.

Bryant would never admit it but he was half in love with the woman because of her cooking.

Keeden liked to tease Bryant that he had mastered an uncanny ability to show up just when one of Mrs. Kayode's dishes did and his friend wasn't far from wrong.

He'd managed to visit Keeden, while he recovered at the Adesina family home after the accident, just after they had received a large serving of stir-fried chicken in a bed of yellow rice from the Kayodes. He helped himself to two servings without any guilt; Mrs. Adesina commenting on his healthy appetite.

He wanted to know her secret but any attempt met with a girlish giggle and deflection. Clearly Mrs. Kayode didn't want to tell him and he didn't blame her. Every meal always made her events a success.

He'd tried many times to replicate the flavors, at times getting close, but never close enough.

But now he had a chance to unravel the truth and he wasn't above using Maya's misdirected infatuation for him to discover a few secrets. He glanced at her as she kept her gaze focused on her plate. The large seven piece tan dining set made her appear smaller than she actually was. Fortunately, he'd managed to convince her to sit across from him widthwise instead of lengthwise.

He cleared his throat and said, "Did you ever learn any of your mother's cooking skills?"

She blinked, swallowed hard (she always seemed to have to gather courage to speak to him, which he found sweet and amusing), before finding her voice. "No, didn't have much interest."

His heart sank. He'd hoped to get some information from her. He'd planned on charming her and slowly extracting what intel he needed but now realized it would be a wasted effort.

"Of course Mom took credit for it all," Maya was saying.

"I'm sorry?" Bryant said annoyed that he'd have to admit to not listening.

"Mom's cooking. I doubt you've ever tasted it."

Bryant frowned. "I've tasted it all the time..." His words fell away as Maya shook her head.

She leaned forward. "I'm going to let you in on a little secret."

He swallowed. This was it. The secret revealed.

"You mustn't tell anyone."

He licked his lip, eagerness coursing through him. "Not a soul," he promised.

"Cat cooks all the meals and Mom takes all the credit."

He blinked. Certain he'd misunderstood her. "I'm sorry. I thought you said Cat."

"I did."

"Cat cooks?"

She nodded.

"Food?"

Maya laughed. "What else would she cook?"

Eye of newt, perhaps? He decided to keep his thoughts to himself. Instead he said, "Not your mother?"

She shook her head. "I doubt Mom even boils water. Let alone salts it. We sometimes joke that buttering toast is beneath her."

He waited. He expected Maya to smile, to burst into laughter and tell him she was joking.

There was no way that Cat, that scary insect of a woman, could be that good a cook.

Not just good, excellent.

The only way he could imagine Cat Kayode wielding a knife was to scare someone with it. He'd once overheard her laughing at a movie image on her cell phone where a guy got an ax through the head.

He refused to believe it. There was no way she could cook with such care, that she could create such long lasting nourishing foods.

"I'm serious," Maya said as if sensing his disbelief. "Everybody knows Cat loves to eat."

Please. Mother of God. This can't be happening.

"But she likes to cook too. Not that she had much choice. Instead of getting a house girl they decided to raise one," Maya said in a rueful tone before she covered her mouth and sent him a guilty look. "Forget I said that. I didn't mean it."

Of course she did, she meant every word, this was the chattiest she'd ever been with him, and he'd didn't care enough to pretend to forget what she'd told him. How could he? It had to be a mistake.

"Are you sure it was Cat? Ava didn't help her?"

"Nope. It's all Cat. Hard to believe I know, but it's the truth."

Bryant felt a little ill, but his curiosity still burned. "Did you...ever watch her? See what she did?"

"No, sorry." She brightened as a thought came to her. "Right. Of course. You like to cook too. Would you like me to ask her—"

"No," he said a bit too quickly. "It's okay." He wanted nothing to do with Cat, even if it would solve a mystery that had haunted him for years. Never ever would he go to her for advice. He'd see that haughty gaze, that serial killer grin. No, he'd stay ignorant.

"She isn't as scary as she seems."

He made a noncommittal sound and picked up his fork then set it back down, his appetite gone. Why did it have to be her? Why? Why!

Maya hesitated. "Are you sure you don't want me to—"

"I'm sure," Bryant said with a note of defeat. Reluctantly remembering the vow he'd made in Arizona.

13

———

THE WINDS of Arizona welcomed him back with a dry, hot kiss. Bryant had never imagined himself back in the state he'd left as a teenager. But a former teacher he'd kept in touch with had managed to get a gallery to show his work. Although he'd never envisioned himself as a gallery artist, his former teacher, a woman who held a keen passion for turquoise jewelry and Brazilian calypso, thought design work was beneath him and a waste of his talent and Bryant said little to argue with her.

However, he'd never have imagined she'd go through the trouble to market his paintings and get a small, yet prestigious gallery to show his work.

The event had turned into a bigger success than he'd imagined and he still wasn't sure who he wanted to be. Someone important, recognized? Well managed? Although those goals felt like they belonged to someone else, he tried to make them his and was determined to enjoy what minor celebrity it afforded him.

He thought of telling Keeden about his change of heart. Keeden was adamantly opposed to being a gallery artist, but Keeden was more of a rebel than Bryant was. Bryant didn't want to offend his former teacher who he respected very much, who'd made an immigrant kid feel welcomed. He had a chance to make his father proud, even perhaps, his mother too.

High art was for the elite. It would put him in a different circle of influence. Perhaps then, with more money and power, he could focus on what he really wanted to do. He was young enough to take this gamble. He was not yet thirty, he still had time.

An autumn rainstorm had left the day cooler than expected so Bryant took the opportunity to leave his hotel and enjoy a leisurely walk around the city.

Mexla wasn't an impressive city; it was barely a city at all. More of a town masquerading as one. It hadn't made a name for itself, like more popular destinations, its main distinguishing feature being a thriving, but academically unremarkable college, so a youthful vibe filled the city with the promise of possibilities, bright futures and new ventures.

He'd found himself walking down a main street still basking in another successful gallery showing and his teacher telling him about the possibility of more. Even better, he wasn't walking alone, an attractive woman whose father had bought two of his paintings walked with him and all the signals she gave him let him know they'd likely spend a wonderful evening together as well. He'd been feeling confident. Successful.

Then he heard a song.

A classical song that swept back the years and embraced him as much as it scared him.

He followed the music and soon found himself in a Mediterranean inspired plaza, whose various buildings boasted red roof tiles and ironwork accents, which gleamed in the sunlight, and saw a small crowd gathered around a young black woman playing the violin. He looked at her. Briefly their eyes met.

He wished they hadn't.

He felt his throat close. His eyes water.

Cat had filled out a little, the teenager now grown into a woman, but not by much.

But her odd sway over him hadn't ebbed.

It was as if she was playing only for him. As calmly as she'd hummed the song all those years ago. Reminding him he was going to be okay; don't be scared.

And yet somehow it scared him more.

His companion's beautifully manicured finger lightly touched his sleeve. "Are you all right?"

He couldn't speak, he couldn't move. He was mesmerized.

Damn you, he wanted to shout at the plain faced woman. Damn you for being here. Damn you for reaching right into me, touching the soft, weak parts I keep buried. How do you do it? How could his angel...no, she'd never been an angel. He'd mistaken her for one. Instead he was certain she'd been touched by a darker power.

One that was dangerous. Destructive.

Briefly, Bryant felt his carefully crafted mask fall, before he was able to settle it back in place. And smile. Always smile. "I'm fine," he said in response to his date's worried expression, "the song just reminded me of something."

His companion frowned, tossing a lock of long brown hair

behind her ear. "She's no Jessie Montgomery. She's barely passable. No wonder she's playing on a street corner."

His first instinct was to defend her. Tell his companion that Cat was far from being as great as the celebrated female violinist and composer, but the notes, the pacing, the vibrato was crisp, clear. She was good. Not great, definitely not brilliant, but she made the song sound like something he'd never heard before and yet comfortably familiar all the same.

Suddenly a solution for a project he'd been working on with Keeden came to him, then an idea for another project he'd been thinking about. She'd unlocked something within him: A wild, free artist unshackled from the weight of obligation and the duties of politeness.

But he didn't like giving her that kind of credit. Didn't like the thought of anyone having such power over him.

Beautifully plain.

Keeden's words from New Jersey rose in his mind. And as Bryant looked at Cat now he saw that perhaps with a touch of color on her lips and eyes, different clothing, perhaps a flowing skirt and southwestern style tunic top instead of the harsh black jeans and shapeless multi-patterned shirt she wore, then she would better match the music she was creating.

But when he looked again he realized he didn't want to touch anything. There was a bold authenticity to how she presented herself to the world. A boldness he didn't have. She didn't mind the criticisms she knew would come.

She played anyway.

~

As if in a trance, Bryant found himself returning to the same spot the following day, partly hoping Cat wouldn't be there.

But she was.

All he had to do was follow the music.

He watched her finish another song then take a bow and begin to put her violin away. He watched every movement—cataloging the curve of her neck, the shape of her legs, her long arms. There was still nothing remarkable about her. The black jeans seemed to make her legs appear skinner and the brown tunic she wore reminded him of rust.

"Are you going to just stand there?" she said after a few moments.

"What?"

She waved at him. "Hello again."

Bryant cleared his throat, heat steeling into his cheeks. "Right, uh hello."

"I thought you were going to pretend not to know me."

"I was."

"What made you change your mind?"

I wish I knew. He shrugged.

"Well, I'm done for the day. You can treat a poor college student to lunch and tell me what you've been up to."

What cheek. To assume that he didn't have something better to do. "I don't want to have lunch with you."

"Okay. Suit yourself." She picked up her violin case and walked away. He stared, stunned, even a little peeved that she didn't appear to be more upset. Why she didn't question his response. Why she didn't find him rude. Instead she just accepted his curt reply and moved on.

He watched her head down a street then turn. He followed.

After a few blocks she stopped suddenly and turned to him. "Are you following me?"

"No." But of course he was and he didn't know why. Didn't know why she intrigued him.

"Want me to treat you to lunch instead?"

"No."

Again that nonchalant shrug. "Suit yourself."

"I will."

It was stupid and completely out of character for him to follow her to a fast food Mexican restaurant and watch her order enough food for three. For a moment he feared she might ask him to join her, but she didn't. She took her large order and sat at one of the square, orange tables and consumed the lot.

He watched in awe. Because she didn't gorge, or attack her food like a ravenous beast, she seemed to enjoy every bite. He felt his stomach grumble and decided to order enchiladas. He didn't expect much, he'd had them plenty of times before.

But this time was different.

The way the Mexican rolls assaulted his senses was almost obscene. The savory flavoring of the tortilla embracing the chicken, how the smooth chile-based sauce mingled with a gooey grilled cheese covering. He'd never experienced it that way before.

All his senses came alive and for a strange, unsettling moment he wanted to share them with her, get her opinion and talk about them and wished he had accepted her invitation.

But no, he was fine. He took another large bite, angered by his wandering thoughts. This was more than good enough. It was heaven. His senses came alive when she was around. Music, no matter how ordinary, seemed to mean more. That's what continued to fascinate him—that the ordinary turned extraordinary in her presence.

When Cat left the restaurant he didn't follow her. But he did wonder when she passed by his table, why she'd said, "Not bad," until he glanced down and realized he'd sketched her, or rather a rendition of her all harsh lines and beady eyes, on a napkin. He crumbled it up and shoved it in his pocket, unable to throw it away. Instead, he discouraged a would-be thief from stealing a woman's purse from her handbag then finished his lunch.

HE SHOWED up at the plaza again, in the same week, one last time he promised himself, and she wasn't there.

He stood in the plaza wondering why he felt so lonely. It wasn't as if he couldn't find her again. He knew her name, who her family was. Keeden could tell him all he needed to know and yet...

Why had he come there in the first place? They weren't friends and he didn't really like her but he liked seeing her; liked hearing her play.

Bryant turned and then saw her running towards him. She raced past him.

"You're late," he said.

She flashed a superior grin. "I know."

Even when he scolded her she made him feel like a peasant.

She had a Band-Aid on her forehead and another on the back of her hand that he didn't want to ask about. He didn't want to care. He wanted to selfishly hear her play and then leave.

"Any requests?" Cat said, tuning the violin.

"No."

"Good, because I don't take them."

"Then why ask?"

The sneaking, harsh grin appeared. "To annoy you."

He didn't ask her why she'd chosen a school in Arizona, one so far from her family; he didn't ask what she was studying. He wasn't interested in any of the polite social niceties expected of him. He didn't feel like being nice to her, she had the ability to bring out the worst side of him.

This dark, angry, emotionally hungry, scared side he didn't want anyone else to see. But something she did, somehow.

"You'll never make it as a professional," he said.

"I know. I gave that up years ago."

Years ago. She made herself sound much older, but she couldn't be more than twenty.

He didn't ask her why she still played when there was no hope for a career. Instead he listened. That's what he'd come there to do.

And as he listened it happened again, the way the music seemed to enter into him, to light the dark, broken cracks of his soul. And he let it. He surrendered.

Then it was over. He turned to leave, renewed.

"Such a waste."

He spun around to her. "I'm sorry?"

"How long are you going to live as a fraud?"

Rage. Boiling rage. He stared down into those cold judging eyes. "You don't know anything about me."

"You got a second chance at life and you're hiding."

She didn't know anything. She certainly didn't know him. "As opposed to what? This? Getting coins of pity?"

Instead of looking hurt, she looked sad. That was infinitely worse.

"I read about you online. I know all about your amazing

gallery show," she made insulting air quotation marks when she said the word amazing, "and I felt like I was reading about somebody else."

"You don't know me," Bryant repeated but his words sounded feeble even to his own ears.

"I know Keeden Adesina. And I know Keeden wouldn't choose a coward as his best friend."

"I'm not a coward."

"Then why are you so afraid of being yourself?"

"I'm not afraid. This is me." He pounded his chest. "I'm trying different opportunities. And...Why am I even explaining this to you? You're still too young to understand how the world works. I'm living my dream."

"You're living someone else's dream."

He held up his hands. "I'm not having this discussion with you. I don't know who you think I am, but you're wrong about me."

"If that's so true why were you flashing that creepy, plastic grin in all of the pictures?"

Creepy? She used that damn word again.

His smile was his weapon, carefully crafted and she thought it was creepy?

He would not argue with her. He had everything. A gallery showing, great reviews, beautiful women (and a few men) who slipped him their info, and all she had was a street corner and a violin. Nothing. She was nothing.

She meant nothing.

Bryant took a deep breath and walked away, feeling her judging gaze burning into his back.

~

THAT GAZE HAUNTED HIS DREAMS, showed up whenever he closed his eyes.

"What put you in such a bad mood?" his companion said, sliding a path down his bare chest.

He'd tried to find solace between her lavender scented thighs, but it hadn't distracted him enough.

He couldn't tell her. He couldn't tell anyone. Because Cat was right. He had been pretending. Damn that little demon. She knew too much. She knew that he was still running scared. Why had he gone back to hear her play? To see her? Why had he made himself vulnerable to her again?

But this was it. The last time.

He did what he did best. He looked at his companion and smiled. Smiled in a way that removed all worry from her pretty face, that reassured her that everything was fine.

But he'd left Arizona soon after and never did another gallery showing, instead he became the graphic designer he'd wanted to be and with Keeden they'd embarked on projects neither could have dreamed of.

THE SQUAWK of a blue jay brought Bryant back to his present life in Maryland. He smiled at Maya, causing her to look both pleased and flustered, and smoothly changed the subject.

What Maya had told him about Cat wouldn't change anything. It only reaffirmed his vow. He'd stay away. He didn't care if he never learned the truth about her delicious meals.

Let it forever remain a mystery.

14

———

Seeing Maya in the kitchen was similar to seeing a mouse dancing around a cat's food bowl: A bad omen.

It was dangerous territory since their mother could show up at any moment and Maya did her best to stay out of her way. It had only been about a week since she'd been staying at Keeden's place. So when Maya entered the kitchen Cat felt all her survival instincts come on high alert.

She was happy to see her. Working with Keeden seemed to have given her more confidence somehow. Her complexion looked brighter, her expression happier.

To give her sister credit she'd scheduled her appearance well. She'd cleverly stopped by when Mom was out for a dress fitting for an upcoming event, but that was still a risky move.

Her sister also looked hopeful and guilty, which meant she wanted something. Cat sighed. She loved her and even though it had been a busy day (she'd had to pick up her father's dry cleaning, inspect a new cloth delivery, look through the wedding registry for a cousin's wedding and make her way through another List) Maya rarely asked for anything special. If Cat could make it happen she would try.

"What do you want?" Cat said, drying her hands on a tea towel. She'd just finished washing the dishes from her quick lunch.

Maya blinked. "Want?"

"Me to cook?" Cat clarified wondering why her sister was acting dense.

"Oh, no that's not why I'm here. It's...I have a favor."

"Okay."

"What do you put on the chicken when you roast it or you know, your other dishes?"

Cat narrowed her eyes. "Why would I tell you that?" She folded her arms, sensing there was something her sister wasn't telling her. "Who wants to know?"

"I do."

Cat sniffed. "No you don't. You want to impress someone by revealing my secrets."

"It's not..." She bit her lip. "I'm sorry. You're right. I did—do want to impress someone."

"Who?"

She lowered her gaze. "It doesn't matter."

"Who?" Cat insisted. Her sister was short and fiesty but at moments like these Maya could make Cat feel as if she'd pulled the fur of a kitten.

Maya tugged on the hem of her jacket, keeping her gaze lowered. "If you knew you wouldn't tell me anyway."

"I might."

"You won't."

"Try me."

Maya paused before she lifted her gaze and said, "Bryant."

Of course, *Bryant*. She should have known. Cat let her arms fall and nodded. "You're right. I won't tell you."

The kitten act disappeared and Maya said, "Why not? What do you have against him?"

"It's what he has against *me*."

Maya frowned. "He hardly knows you. You're the one who always teases him..." She paused. "I know there's something about him you don't like. I can't imagine what it is. I mean he's friendly, successful, kind and sometimes, when that accent of his slips through..." Her expression turned dreamy. "Oh, it's so nice. What could possibly bother you about him?"

"How much time do you have?"

"That's not funny."

"I'm not trying to be funny. Why would I tell him?"

"Because he's curious. I told him about you."

"Why would you tell him about me?"

"I don't know," Maya said with a guilty laugh. "It's hard for me to talk to him and it just, I don't know, fell out."

"Fell out?" Cat said in a flat tone.

Maya nodded. "Yeah. He asked me about Mom's cooking and I was trying to be clever and...I know, I know I shouldn't have but I did and," she sighed. "Don't worry I made him promise not to tell anyone. But he looked so," her expression turned wistful as she thought about him. Cat did her best not to gag. "I want to help him. And it might increase my chances with him if I buttered him up a bit."

"So you're still interested in him."

"Of course I am," she said surprised. "W-why wouldn't I be?"

Cat shrugged. "I just thought things might have changed now that you're working with Keeden."

Maya's dreamy expression and light tone turned to stone. "Nothing's changed with Keeden," Maya said in a cold, flat voice.

Cat stared at her sister for a long moment, sensing a lie, but she wouldn't push it. "Okay."

After a moment Maya said in a shy voice, "So you won't tell me?"

"No."

"He didn't ask me to do this so don't mention it to him, please."

"But it would be so much fun to torture him."

"Cat."

"Just a little."

Maya pressed her hands together. "Please."

"I'll think about it."

"Cat, I mean it. Don't use his curiosity against him."

She playfully motioned to the kitchen exit as if dismissing a servant. "You may go now."

Maya scowled. "Is there any way I can—"

"No."

"I don't know what it is between you two."

"Hmm."

"If we start dating, you'll be nice to him, right?"

Cat gave a noncommittal nod. She felt a little sad that her sister still remained so hopeful. She didn't have a chance with Bryant, because he wasn't the man she thought he was.

But that night, to her annoyance, Cat couldn't stop thinking about Maya's request.

Bryant was curious about her cooking, huh? That gave her a strange thrill. She delighted in the idea—reveled in how much it must bother him—that he couldn't figure it out.

She wouldn't divulge all her secrets, she had a few, but she had one that could offer him a hint.

It would be fun to offer him a challenge.

15

THE TRUTH COULD BE a bitter pill.

And Bryant had to swallow it every day.

Cat cooked.

And he loved her cooking.

But when he learned that Cat and Ava were stopping by to visit with their sister Maya, Bryant performed his famous disappearing act.

Keeden might have to endure their visit for appearances sake but he certainly didn't. Fortunately, Keeden's house was large, so hiding wasn't difficult.

No one managed to find him until the sisters had gone.

Bryant waited until he knew they were safely away—their car out of sight—before he emerged from his hiding place.

He was safe.

He entered the kitchen proud of his success then paused when he saw a medium size jar left on the counter. He cautiously crept closer and saw a note addressed to him. It read: *Bryant, Here's a clue. Cat*

He lifted the glass bottle and studied the strange white and red mixture inside. He twisted open the bottle and wince as the pungent scents escaped. Something tangy, fermented and spicy assaulted his nose-scents that felt both familiar and exotic.

The note didn't tell him what the mixture was, but he felt closer now to understanding her cooking than he'd ever been. His heart began to race as he thought of finally being able to replicate those sensational savory flavors.

He put the jar in the fridge and planned to try it out the following day.

But it mysteriously disappeared.

He stood in front of the fridge and let the appliance's cold breath chill his skin. He refused to believe it.

He emptied out the entire fridge. Louise Nyugen, Keeden's cook found him searching through the items he'd crowded on top of the kitchen island and counters.

"What are you doing?"

He briefly glanced at the older woman with purple highlights in her short black hair. "My jar. I have to find my jar."

"What jar?"

He turned to her hopeful. She must have moved it. "Have you seen a little glass jar with a yellow cap?"

She nodded. "It looked like something rotten, and smelled even worse, so I threw it out."

Bryant rushed to the garbage hoping she'd thrown it out intact.

"I poured the contents down the disposal and cleaned the jar," she said, dashing that hope.

He closed his eyes and groaned.

"Did I do something wrong?"

He kept his eyes closed. It would really be a bad look if he started to tear up. He struggled to keep his voice light, pretend it didn't matter. "It was for a recipe."

"I'm sorry. Keeden usually doesn't keep things like that. I thought it was food he'd forgotten."

"Fair enough." Bryant opened his eyes and began to put the items back in the fridge. "It was my fault for not labeling it."

"I'll get you the ingredients to try it again."

If only he knew what they were.

"It's okay."

But it wasn't okay. After he'd finished restocking the fridge, Bryant went to his room and paced and swore and swore and swore. Now he'd never know. He couldn't ask her again. Couldn't tell her that he'd been careless with her 'gift'. He didn't want to admit that he cared.

He swore again. He'd gotten so close to what he'd wanted and yet again it'd slipped through his fingers.

He hung his head.

Little knowing that more than a month later Maya and Keeden would be a couple, his house renovations would finish on time (and on budget) and fate would give him another chance.

16

———

Bryant would never imagine it would take a windy day, a hanging spider plant and a stepstool to summon a witch.

His father had summoned her innocently, as he did most things.

His father had left the windows open and was adjusting the hanging plant when a gush of wind had caused him to lose his balance and topple off his stepstool.

Thankfully, he didn't fall frequently, but when he did, he did it spectacularly. He ended up hitting the side of his face and bruising his clavicle. Fortunately, Gareth had gone to check on him when he hadn't shown up at the rec center and had convinced him to get treated.

Bryant invited his father to come and stay with him for a few days and, more embarrassed than in pain, his father agreed. But news of the event travelled fast and soon visitors arrived.

That's how Cat happened to end up at Bryant's house.

A place she'd never been before.

A place he'd never wanted her to be.

When it came to delivering things, the Kayodes usually sent Ava. She was the sweetest of the sisters and Bryant liked her, but he'd learned she was busy. Gwen was away and he couldn't think of anytime she ran an errand so he dismissed that possibility. Maya would have been the next logical choice, but he'd heard from Keeden that she'd been kicked out of the house because Mrs. Kayode blamed her for Ava's broken engagement or something weird like that, so they'd sent the last one.

The last one he'd ever wanted to see.

Bryant opened the front door with all the enthusiasm of an undertaker.

He didn't smile at Cat and she didn't smile at him. She just nodded to the square glass container she held, letting him know she'd been ordered to deliver food, and he would have taken it from her and closed the door, if his father hadn't come down the hall and welcomed her inside as if she were an esteemed guest.

She shoved the container in his chest, enough to make him wince; surprised she'd carried what felt like a cement filled boulder so easily, before she turned her attention to his father. She fussed over his bandage and made him laugh. Bryant growled and went into the kitchen and shoved the container in the fridge and slammed the door.

In five minutes she'd grow bored and then leave.

But five minutes passed and she was still there. He folded his arms and leaned against the counter.

She was still there fifteen minutes later.

When twenty minutes had passed Bryant left the kitchen and went to the living room where he thought he'd find them.

But they weren't there. He went to the patio.

They weren't there either.

When he returned inside he heard laughter floating from upstairs. He followed the sound and found them basked in sunlight.

They both sat on the window seat. It was one of the renovations Bryant had designed for his father. For the first time the room looked exactly as he'd hoped it would: A comfortable alcove for his father to enjoy when he came to visit. The room had a large window for him to look out of, a sitting area, as well as the window seat. His father looked at home.

His father had a hardback book opened on his lap and Cat was leaning forward nodding at whatever he was saying. She said something and made his father laugh. Really laugh. Few people could do that. They'd been reunited years ago at one of Keeden's events and his father had recognized Cat immediately. However, for reasons of his own, his father also had never told anyone of how they'd first met. Therefore, how their lives had intertwined in Georgia that fateful day remained a secret only they shared.

Bryant strained to hear what Cat continued to say to keep his father smiling. What kind of spell had she put him under? He looked different. More alert and yet wistful. Young. Perhaps the fall had been more serious than they'd first thought?

The tenderness in which she approached and talked to his father shocked him. Touched him. Most people treated his father as if he were a child, or damaged, but Cat let him keep his dignity even if he repeated a statement one time too many.

Bryant felt his heart shift.

Then quickly took back control of it.

No, he wouldn't be swayed by that, swayed by her. There could be nothing good getting involved with a woman like that.

His father looked up and motioned him forward. "This is my son, Bryant."

"Yes," Cat said in a gentle and patient voice he didn't know she was capable of, "I know."

"Of course you know," his father said with a firm nod, reminding himself of things he knew he ought to remember, "You've known each other a long time."

"Yes."

"And you love each other."

"No!" they both cried in unison, sharing a look of horror.

His father trembled, violently shaken from their outburst.

Cat touched his hand. "I'm sorry. I didn't mean to shout, but we're not close like that. You must be confusing me with someone else."

He frowned. "Aren't you the little girl who saved our lives?"

"Yes, but that was a very long time ago and you've both thanked me for it more than you know."

He took her hand. "I love you."

"I love you too." She stood. "And now I should go so you can get some rest."

His father rushed to his feet. "I'm making you leave."

"No," Cat said quickly, "I wish I could stay, but it's really time I go."

His gaze shifted from her face to Bryant's then back again. He sensed the tension in the air. "I said something wrong, didn't I?"

Bryant could see his father was getting anxious and probably convincing Cat to stay would ease it, but selfishly he really wanted her gone.

"It's okay, Dad. She'll come back again."

His face brightened. "Soon?"

"Yes." It was a smooth lie. Sometimes his father could be easily distracted and would quickly forget he'd wanted her to come again.

Cat left the room, making sure to bump him with her shoulder when she walked past him. Bryant resisted the urge to bump her back.

"Aren't you going to show her out?" his father said as they heard her footsteps descend the stairs.

"She knows the way," Bryant said, knowing he was disappointing his father by being rude, but unable to muscle up the energy to care. Instead he headed to the kitchen to make his father a snack.

He opened the fridge and paused at the sight of Cat's glass dish. In the past, he would have eaten it right away, knowing it would be delicious.

But now he hesitated because he knew the truth—Mrs. Kayode hadn't made it. Cat had.

He started to close the fridge then stopped. One bite.

He tore off the lid and separated a tiny piece with a fork. He took a bite and moaned with pleasure, savoring the crispy edges and creamy center; the touch of lemon the array of herbs.

One tiny bite turned into two then three before the fritter was gone.

He softly swore, covered the container and pushed it back into the fridge.

"What are you doing?" his father asked, coming into the room.

Bryant spun around feeling guilty. What had he come in here for again? Right... "I was making you a snack."

His father waved him away. "Don't make me anything. I'm not hungry."

"Okay." He frowned. If he wasn't hungry, why was he in the kitchen? "Did you need something?"

"Shame she had to go. I really like her."

"I know you do."

"She smells nice and is really kind."

"Hmm." He wasn't sure about that.

"I really like her."

This was one of the times when his father's habit of repeating things could grate on his nerves. He'd likely have to hear the statement repeated six more times before his father moved on to something else. His father had improved over the years but there were still times, like this when he was upset or there was a major change, when it was hard.

Bryant opened the cupboard, perhaps some tea would soothe him.

"Beautiful eyes."

He turned sharply to his father. That wasn't like him to expand on a topic this long and he couldn't be talking about her. But he didn't see him looking at a magazine, or a phone, and there was no TV in the kitchen, maybe it was just a random thought that had entered his head. "Who has beautiful eyes?"

"Cat."

"No, she doesn't. She doesn't have beautiful anything."

If he wasn't certain he would have thought his father looked at him with pity before he looked away.

"I hope she comes back soon," he said.

"Hmm."

"I really like her." He patted Bryant on the shoulder. "We both do."

Bryant bit back a response. "You should go rest."

His father nodded and left without argument.

Bryant inwardly sighed relieved that he was now alone at last. His father was fine and the woman was gone.

He turned to leave and saw a figure standing there.

17

———

HE SCREAMED.

It wasn't his proudest moment. To scream at the sight of a slip of a woman as if he'd come upon an ax murderer. His fright quickly turned into anger.

Bryant glared at her. "What the hell are you doing here?"

"I'm sorry," Cat said, not sounding sorry at all, her eyes dancing with malicious delight. "I came back to ask you something but then...I didn't want to disturb you."

She didn't want to disturb him? How long had she been hiding there? What did she mean? And then he remembered guiltily indulging in the leafy green fritters. His face burned with the acute humiliation of a teenager caught masturbating.

"And then your father came into the kitchen," Cat continued with a knowing grin, "and I didn't want him to see me so I hid until he left and I did clear my throat, but clearly you didn't hear me."

"What do you want?" he ground out, his jaw so tight it ached.

"Did you figure it out?"

"What?"

"The flavoring. You did get the jar, didn't you?"

"Yes."

"And…"

"No, I didn't figure it out." *But I didn't because the mixture got thrown out and I don't want to tell you that.*

She shrugged. "Too bad. I thought you would have." She turned. "Bye."

She was walking away. He liked seeing her do that, he liked it even better when she disappeared out of the room, but then she was taking the secret with her and he really wanted to know. He was close and it was worth a little pain to get to the truth.

"I didn't get a chance," Bryant called after her.

Silence greeted his words.

Just as he thought she'd already left, Cat peeked her head inside and sent him a quizzical look. "What was that?"

He sighed, hating having to repeat it. "I didn't get a chance to…uh…test it."

She walked back into the kitchen and folded her arms. "Why not?"

"Louise threw it out."

"Who?"

"Keeden's chef."

"Oh right. I see."

Cat looked at him for a long moment and he thought she would be upset instead she threw her head back and laughed loud and hard.

"Really?" she gasped, wiping tears from her eyes.

He nodded.

She slapped her thigh and laughed harder.

Bryant folded his arms. "I don't know what you find so funny."

She pointed at him. "You."

"Me?"

"I can just imagine the look on your face when you discovered..." She laughed some more.

It was just like her to find amusement in his misery. He would endure this. Get the secret and then never need anything from her ever again.

"It's been more than a month," she finally said, managing to compose herself. "Why didn't you say anything?"

"I'm saying it now."

"You still want to know?"

"Yes," he said in a clipped voice.

"I'll make you another mixture."

"Just tell me what it is."

"Where would the fun be in that?"

"I don't want fun."

She sent him a sly look. "I think you do. But I could show you something real quick right now. Your father will love it."

His father had said he wasn't hungry, but Bryant knew that sometimes his father pretended not to be hungry in order not to bother him. He hesitated.

She noticed. "What is it?"

"I don't like people in my kitchen—"

She made a move to leave. "Okay."

"—but I'll make an exception this one time."

Cat gave him a curtsey, that felt like a giant rude gesture. "Thank you, Your Majesty."

He frowned.

"I wasn't dressed to cook do you mind if I..." She gestured to his apron hanging near the pantry door.

Bryant hesitated again then gave a curt nod.

But the apron was enormous on her so she had to wrap the belt around her waist twice to keep it in place.

He stood a safe distance away and watched her like a prison guard would a convict. He watched her grab some left-over chicken and instant noodles and quickly guessed what she was planning to make. When she reached for garlic, ginger and soy sauce, his suspicions were confirmed.

He studied how she moved around his kitchen with a strange familiarity, rarely faltering when she needed something.

"Have you been in here before when I wasn't around?" he asked.

"No, I can guess how you think."

That was definitely unsettling but she was probably hinting that he was a boring cook and he didn't feel in the mood to argue.

She ordered him to chop some broccoli and peppers, which he didn't expect. Fortunately, the kitchen was large enough for him to keep his distance from her.

But as he rhythmically chopped the peppers, listened to the sizzling of oil and smelled the fragrant scents of ginger and roasted garlic he thought of how Cat had made his father laugh, how patient and kind she'd been to him. Then he remembered his father's words. *Beautiful eyes. She smells nice. I love her.*

And he remembered how briefly his heart had softened towards her, how when she'd bumped into him, he'd been tempted by her scent—an orange and jasmine mix with a sultry essence that lingered on her skin, and he'd wanted to bump her back, his body craving more. Which made no sense. He gripped the knife handle tighter. It didn't matter how good she smelled or how much his father liked her. "I'm not going to fall in love with you."

"I didn't expect you to," she said.

Bryant paused startled, "What?"

"I don't expect you to fall in love with me," Cat said.

He softly swore. "Sorry. Didn't mean to say that out loud." He usually didn't have other people around him when he cooked. Cooking helped him to think and he had a bad habit of talking aloud to himself when he did.

"I guessed that," Cat said amused. "Don't worry, I didn't imagine you offering your first born in exchange for my secrets. And I know your father means well."

"Hmm."

Mercifully, she let the subject drop and returned to cooking.

Within minutes the tantalizing aroma of the chicken stir-fry with noodles lured his father into the kitchen.

"Something smells delicious," he said then stopped and beamed in delight when he saw Cat. "Oh, you're back!"

"Yes," she said, returning his smile. "Bryant was making something very special for you."

Bryant glanced at her surprised by the lie, but she pointedly avoided his gaze.

"You must stay and eat with us," his father said.

"Another time." She untied the apron and hung it up before she turned to Bryant. "I'll be by next week. I'll let you know before I drop by."

He could only nod annoyed that he looked forward to it.

18

____

She'd lied.

It'd take her nearly two weeks to return and even though she'd sent him a text to tell him the change in plans he was no less annoyed when he opened the door and saw her standing there, casually holding a jar in her hand.

A devious eagerness seized him and he half expected to hiss, "My precious," before snatching the jar and closing the door in her face.

But he didn't. He'd remain cordial because, unfortunately, he still needed her.

Cat held the jar out to him. "Here you go."

He opened the door wider. "Come in."

"Why would I come in?"

"So you can show me."

She lifted her brows. "How to open a jar?"

"No," Bryant said with waning patience, "how to use the ingredient."

"Don't you want to figure it out on your own?"

"No."

She made a face. "That's no fun."

"I know."

"Then I don't need to show you. I'll write instructions with all the joy of a technical report. Will that suit you?"

"No." He motioned towards the kitchen. "Go on."

She put the jar in his hand. "I said figure it out."

"I don't want to." He put the jar back in her hand. "I want you to show me."

"You'll find out for yourself." She stared at him confused. "Don't you want that triumph?"

"No," he shot back. "I don't want to have to see you again."

She blinked. "Oh."

He sighed. "I didn't mean it like that."

"Yes, you did."

"I mean." He took a deep breath. "I'd like to get this over with."

She nodded. "Like a dentist visit or a trip to the urologist?"

He nodded in agreement. "Something like that."

"Then I'll make it swift. All you have to do is—"

He covered her mouth with his hand. "I said *show* me."

She glared at him.

He removed his hand and motioned down the hall. "Go on."

She stared at him for a long moment then she began to smile. The smile made his blood run cold but he still didn't anticipate what she did next.

She lifted the jar then released her grip and let it smash against the ground. She spun on her heel and walked towards her car.

Bryant followed her, squinting against the glare of the summer sun, his outrage making the sun's rays feel like his skin was being blasted by lasers. "What is wrong with you?"

Cat stopped so suddenly he nearly bumped into her. He quickly stumbled back as she turned to glare at him. "Me? Who do you think you are ordering me like a servant? I did this as a favor and you don't even have the decency to play along even a little bit? You don't deserve to know. So you're free. You don't have to see me again unless you're unlucky enough to bump into me at one of the events. I'll do my best to stay out of your way. Actually, I don't have to." She poked him in the chest. "Because I can always send you running."

"I admit it." He wiped sweat from his forehead. "I don't like you. You scare me, alright? But cooking is important to me and I don't want to get this wrong. I don't think I will be able to figure it out and the thought that I'd have to—"

"To come and ask me would wound your pride too much," she finished. "I get it. I really do, but I still thought you were made of stronger stuff. I've never shared this mixture with anyone. And you're still such a coward."

Her words stung, but this time he didn't care because she was right and he wouldn't fight it. "I'm sorry," he said quickly, hoping he could get her to forgive him enough to give him another chance. "Make me another mixture and I will figure it out. I promise."

Cat sent him one of her inscrutable looks before she opened her car door and simply said, "I don't want to," before she slammed the door shut and drove away.

He deserved that. He shouldn't have acted like a bully. She'd graciously made the mixture for him again and he'd been rude. But he'd also been honest. He was scared and a part of him didn't want to disappoint her. She seemed so certain he'd figure out how to use it and if he failed, that would wound his pride more than anything else. But he'd never admit it. She was younger than him by almost a decade and although he was good looking and successful and she wasn't, she could reduce him to a puddle of nerves. It was humiliating.

He wiped more beads of sweat from his forehead and went back inside. His father stood in the foyer.

"I heard a crash," he said.

"I'm sorry about that," Bryant said, welcoming the coolness of the house. He closed the front door eager to escape the sun's bright penetrating gaze. "I'll clean it up."

"What happened?" His father wrinkled his nose and looked at the mess. "What is that?"

Bryant stared down at the shattered jar and its contents, which spilled out like the insides of a carcass; it smelled just as foul too.

What is that? He wasn't sure how to answer him. "My hope. My pride. You name it."

His father frowned confused. "What?"

"Never mind."

Bryant went to the cupboard to get gloves and cleaning supplies, reliving the moment in the driveway. The look in Cat's eyes. They were a shocking brown, fringed with short, dark lashes he'd never noticed before and they were filled with a passion that shook him.

Cat hadn't only been angry with him, but he saw a lingering sadness, as if he'd hurt her feelings. He'd never imagined he'd have the capability. He never imagined that she had feelings at all.

But somehow, unintentionally, he'd hurt her and that bothered him more than he cared to admit.

He'd gotten his wish. She wouldn't step foot in his house again.

And he'd never felt more depressed.

19

CAT WAS angrier at herself than she could ever be with Bryant. She'd revealed too much about herself. He now knew he was special: That he'd been the only person who'd been able to convince her to share one of her secrets.

That must have polished his oversized ego. No doubt he was used to women doing things for him. That's why he'd been so confident he could boss her around.

Cat slowed her car at a traffic light and berated herself.

Why did she lose her temper? Would it have been so hard to have just shown him? Then she could have worked in that wonderful kitchen of his again.

His kitchen was just like the man—big, dark, handsome. She never imagined black cabinetry would work, she expected them to feel intimidating and cold, but the kitchen's steel accents and light hardwood floor, blending with the room's sleek design made it feel warm and inviting. She'd enjoyed cooking there.

And she should have left it at that. She should have done what he'd told her. He was older than she was and she should have treated him with the respect their community expected to be given to people of his age and status.

Cat noticed the light change and pressed her foot against the gas.

This was bad.

She could get into a lot of trouble if anyone knew the informal and rude way she'd treated him. One complaint to Keeden and the treatment of his best friend could be used as a slight or insult to the Adesinas and Cat could find herself facing the punishment of the elders. Bryant could make her life a misery.

But she knew he wouldn't. He'd pretend nothing happened like he pretended about most things.

That thought didn't make her feel any better. She should never have tried to help him. She'd been foolish to think they could have fun. That she could unlock the real Bryant she'd only managed to see glimpses of.

She'd gotten away with treating him different because he was different. His black British father made him an outsider, not fully Nigerian. And he didn't know—hadn't been taught—the power of the social currency he still held. He could have easily used his mother's Nigerian connections to his advantage or even his own present status as a successful designer and entrepreneur. At times she found him as naïve as a toddler with a bar of gold—he didn't know the value of what he had.

But he did know how to get his own way.

Why should he follow her rules anyway?

Because the game would have been fun, an impish voice said. She would have liked to have heard about his attempts. She knew Bryant was one person who not only enjoyed cooking, but eating too. Keeden frequently joked about how much his friend appreciated food.

He'd take care to use the mixture in creative ways, perhaps there could have been something she could have learned from him.

He might have used it in a way she never had considered before. Sharing the mixture with him had felt like embarking on a grand adventure or like being two scientists trying to achieve something.

But she meant nothing to him except a means to an end. She knew he didn't like her. She'd never considered how much.

I admit it. I'm scared of you.

That's what he'd said. To her face! With all the angst and shame of a supplicant at a confessional.

What was there to be scared of?

Sure, she knew how to push his buttons, get under his skin, and she wasn't pretty to look at, but did that truly make her terrifying?

She should let him wonder.

Let him linger in defeat.

It would be a tiny victory.

But a hollow one. Bryant Meadows was a fraud. It wasn't his fault she'd wanted him to be more.

She'd called him a coward, but she knew he wasn't one. Not in the way that mattered. She'd seen evidence of it over the past few years but the most memorable had been in Arizona.

He'd amused her by following her to a restaurant then drawing a picture of her on a napkin. She'd left the restaurant first but glanced at him through the window just as she saw him tense. She followed his gaze and saw him staring at a man reaching his hand into a woman's purse.

Her gaze darted back to Bryant and she saw him utter the words, 'You don't want to do that.'

The man turned sharply and stared at him.

Bryant didn't just stare back; his eyes glinted in a welcome challenge as if daring the man to give him a reason to act. His gaze promising a painful confrontation.

The man hurried out of the restaurant.

Cat had to stop herself from plastering her hands and face against the glass, stunned by his transformation. *That* was Bryant Meadows?

The look he'd given the other man was a good guy move but held a bad guy vibe. Cat wasn't sure if Bryant had wanted to stop the woman from getting her purse stolen or if he'd taken more pleasure in threatening the would-be thief.

He acted mild, but he had the instincts of a fighter. She could picture him as one of her favorite wrestlers making an opponent beg for mercy.

At first she would have cast him as a babyface, a good guy, never imagining him as a heel, a bad guy, but that quick, menacing glare put him in the rare category of a tweener—a character who refused to be pigeon-holed as either good or bad. It wasn't an easy role to play, but a fun one to watch because you never knew what to expect from them: A sneak attack from behind, a well-executed body slam.

He'd be poetry in motion.

Bryant's predator instincts were still on high alert and he must have sensed her staring, because he began to turn towards the window.

Cat darted out of sight before he saw her. She staggered away in breathless awe, her heart pounding.

He may not like to be scared, but he could instill it in others—and knew how.

Later that day, she invented a nickname (Death-Hunter) and an entire storyline for him and imagined him involved in a casket match, where the objective was to trap the opposing wrestler in a casket. She choreographed all the maneuvers he'd do to win.

So inspired by him, and her feverish imagination, she'd tried a wrestling move she probably shouldn't have and had ended up nearly knocking herself out.

The following day, Bryant had surprised her by showing up again at the plaza and she'd been embarrassed to have him see her with a bandage on her forehead and hand, but, to her relief, he was too polite (or didn't care) to ask about them.

But she hadn't seen that man in the Mexican restaurant again. He kept that side of himself buried under thick layers of charm and easy smiles or simple power plays, like the one he conducted today.

Cat let her shoulders sag.

She'd give the bully what he wanted. What did it matter anyway? What little respect she'd had for him had dwindled. At least Maya was no longer fawning over him so how she treated him wouldn't increase or harm Maya's chances. He was merely a family acquaintance. Her sister's boyfriend's best friend.

By doing him a favor he'd be indebted to her and she could show she was the more mature one in spite of how highly he thought of himself.

That should take him down a peg or two.

The thought made her smile.

20

———

THE PACKAGE LOOKED HARMLESS, which didn't explain why Bryant had been staring at it for the past ten minutes.

He remembered finding it on his doorstep, reading the return label and knowing it was from Cat.

He remembered carefully setting it on his kitchen counter and taking a step back.

And not moving.

It had been a week since his last encounter with her, he hadn't expected this.

He wasn't a big fan of surprises.

Especially from her.

Bryant grabbed a pair of scissors and crossed over to the box then set the scissors down and folded his arms.

What if it wasn't the jar? What if it was something else? A prank? Then again, What if it *was* the jar? What did that mean?

He picked up his phone and sent a text. *Thanks got the package.*

He'd just set the phone down when she sent a reply.

Have you opened it yet?

No.

Then aren't you thanking me too soon? It could be something nasty.

He nodded amused and typed: *You read my mind*, before he quickly deleted it and typed instead: *Like what?*

I can list them in alphabetical order or by level or gruesomeness.

I just opened the box.

<angry cat sticker> You really are no fun.

He chuckled, finding the cat imagine cute. *I told you I don't like being scared.*

<pouty cat sticker>

I forgive you.

<shocked cat sticker> What!

For stinking up my foyer and covering it with scattered glass.

I hope you pricked your finger and bled.

I did.

<thumbs up image>

You really are mean.

<cat smiling>

He grinned in spite of himself. *Thanks again.*

You'll figure it out.

And if I don't?

She didn't reply. She left his text unread.

Bryant decided not to read too much into that. He'd gotten what he'd wanted. That was all that mattered now.

He carefully took the jar out of the carefully packaged box and immediately put it in the fridge. She'd given him another chance. His heart swelled with relief. Finally he could figure out the secret and he would. Somehow she'd given him confidence. Perhaps she hadn't replied because the text didn't deserve one.

The following day he took the jar out of the fridge, stared at it and his mind went blank. Completely blank.

"That's never happened before," he said aloud.

Every time he took out meat, poultry, fish even vegetables and then took out the jar to experiment, he froze. What was this strange feeling? He'd never hesitated before. Maybe because it was too precious. Perhaps because there wasn't enough of it and he didn't want to experiment and use it all up and still not uncover the mystery. Whatever the reason, he couldn't move on.

He softly swore then sent her a text. *Give me a hint*

To his surprise she replied right away. *No.*

He frowned. Adding the full stop punctuation was just rude. *Come on A tiny one.*

No.

Please The sample's small and I don't want to waste it.

Start with chicken.

Yes, that was good. *A good tip. Got plenty.*

But he froze again. Sent another text: *Baked? Fried? Broiled? Grilled? Stir fried?*

Pick one.

What would you pick?

She didn't reply. He didn't blame her. He put the mixture back in the fridge. He'd get to it another time.

An hour later he was working on a sketch in his studio when someone rang the doorbell.

But 'rang' was too gentle a term. Someone assaulted the

doorbell making the usually gently ringing chimes scream like alarm sirens.

He swore loudly and swung the door open, ready to unleash his anger, but stopped when he saw Cat's sly grin.

21

—————

"I should have known," Bryant said, leaning against the doorframe, surprised that his annoyance had quickly turned to joy. He shouldn't be this happy to see her. But he kept his face and voice neutral. "What are you doing?"

Cat shrugged and said with playful disgust, "Helping out a coward." She pushed past him, briefly enchanting him with a fragrant scent his body seemed determined to respond to, and walked through the door. "You win," she said, "I'll show you."

Yes! Success! He'd won! If he wasn't careful, he'd grab her and kiss her. He cleared his throat and folded his arms instead, "Okay."

Cat walked into the kitchen and put on his apron then washed her hands.

"How's your dad?"

"Fine, he'll be visiting soon."

"Good." She dried her hands and her conversational tone turned formal and serious. "I'm going to show you a chicken dish."

He sniffed. "Chicken, huh? Did you choose that because you think I'm a coward?"

"No, I chose it because you mentioned it in your text." She grinned. "However, you're right. It's fitting." She made a flapping motion with her arms. He rolled his eyes.

She pointed at him. "Now watch closely and follow what I do."

He nodded. "Get on with it then."

He stayed a safe distance away and tried to mimic her every move.

She was slow and methodical and a good teacher. She answered every question and never made him feel stupid as he'd suspected she would.

She carefully explained the big tasks and gave him proper distance for the smaller ones, letting him decide several choices to make because she wanted him to keep his own style.

Finally, they put their two efforts in the stove. "In about an hour you'll be done."

"Thank you."

She nodded.

"Where are you going?" he asked as she untied the apron and hung it up. "Don't you want to taste the results?"

"Not really."

"You shouldn't abandon your pupil at the most critical moment."

"My pupil got to cheat."

"I didn't want to waste even a tiny drop."

She pointed to the jar on the counter top. "You notice you still have some left?"

"I wouldn't have without your help." He rested his hands on his hips. "Come on, you've got to stay and see how it turns out."

She hesitated. "An hour is a long time."

"I think I can find us something to do," he said, although that was a lie. He wouldn't know what to do with her.

As if sensing his desperation, Cat said, "No, that's okay. I'll be back. I've got some errands to do."

That was also a lie and she was glad he didn't stop her.

She really didn't treasure the thought of enduring an hour in his presence. She was still annoyed with herself for coming over. But she didn't regret the sight of joy that had briefly lit his expression when she'd said she'd help him.

Cat left and Bryant returned to his studio but he couldn't focus. Would she come back? Had he finally figured it out? Why had he tried to convince her to stay? That was completely out of character. And why had he been disappointed when she'd turned him down?

It was the anticipation, he tried to convince himself. He wanted to get this right. That's why. It had nothing to do with her.

He didn't need her.

WHEN CAT RETURNED, fifteen minutes before the oven timed, she was kinder to the doorbell, giving it a brief tap, making the sound of her arrival a welcome one.

Bryant swung open the door then frowned at the sight of the reusable bags she carried. She didn't say anything as she walked past him and headed to the kitchen.

He watched her confused while she opened the pantry door.

"What are you doing?" he finally said.

"I saw you were running low on some items and I thought

since I was already at the store I'd pick some up for you. You mentioned your father was scheduled for another visit and I know how much he loves this." She waved a jar of Ovaltine before she put it on the shelf and then a second one.

"You bought two," he said confused.

She sent him a sly grin. "Because I'm assuming he's not the only one who enjoys it." She also put a can of sweet milk, English tea and a box of chocolate digestives and shortbread cookies next to it. Bryant blinked surprised by the thought that she could actually be kind of...sweet.

And an overwhelming, unwanted feeling washed over him again. A desire to pull her into his arms and kiss her in gratitude; hug her in relief that she'd considered something that had escaped him; and hold her close for a reason that made no sense at all.

Horror soon followed. What the hell was he thinking? No, no, no. Not that. He didn't want that. Ever.

Bryant gripped his hands into a fist angered by his traitorous thoughts, his traitorous body, and his traitorous gaze that lingered on the curve of her neck, the curve of her backside, the shape of her long fingers, wondering what they would feel like sliding down his chest...

Shit.

Bryant stepped away with such haste he nearly tripped over his own feet.

He would not succumb to this beady eyed little devil that still, at times, reminded him of the peace given to him by his ugly little angel and even more briefly, more dangerously reminded him of a woman with a tender heart, who he could trust, who he could...

No, not her. Anyone but her.

Cat looked at him with concern. "Is something wrong?"

Everything! "I've got uh...I'll be right back." Bryant turned. He had to force himself not to run; when he entered his studio he had to force himself not to slam the door.

He paced his studio and pounded his chest with his fist, hoping the pain would stop his wayward thoughts, his responsive body. He would *not* fall for her. It didn't matter that she was kind to his father, even considerate of him.

He couldn't stand the thought of surrendering to her power. To her sway. She could hurt him in a way no one else could. Her opinion of him already wasn't high.

God, if she knew, how she'd laugh.

The thought of her haughty laughter, cooled his mind and helped him regain control.

He took a deep, steadying breath. It was just a moment of weakness. He'd had a lot on his mind and he was hungry. That was it. He just needed food.

Feeling more relaxed he left his studio.

On his walk back to the kitchen he heard humming and water splashing. He walked into the kitchen and found Cat at the sink cleaning up the dishes.

He took the power of his simmering unwelcomed desire and turned it into rage.

What the hell was she doing!! She wasn't supposed to be nice. She wasn't supposed to be caring. She wasn't supposed to look so perfect standing there in his kitchen, wiggling her skinny little body as if she was having a good time. What game was she playing?

"Stop that," Bryant half shouted, half begged.

Cat turned quickly, startled. "I was just—"

"I only asked you for one thing. You don't have to buy things or clean up or anything else. Do you understand?"

"No."

Of course she'd make this difficult. "I don't like people in my kitchen and—"

Cat pulled off the gloves, which didn't take much effort since they were too large for her. "And I've made myself a bit too comfortable."

"Yes."

She stared at him for a long moment before she turned her back to him, pulled on the oversized gloves and began washing again.

He stared baffled then said, "What are you doing?"

"I'm finishing what I started."

"I told you—"

"I heard you the first time."

"Then why—" This time a handful of suds smashed into his face stopping his words.

"Shut up you ungrateful cow," she said. "I'll be done in a minute."

Cow? Did she just call him a cow? Bryant wasn't sure if his body trembled from anger, surprise, humiliation or, god help him, amusement.

He wiped his face. Counted to five then grabbed the back of her neck causing her to cry out in surprise. He bent down and whispered, "When I tell you to leave, I mean it." He then led her out of the kitchen and released her before he turned.

He shouldn't have done that. By the time he heard the footsteps it was too late. She'd jumped on his back and wrapped her arms around his neck.

He reached for her arm. "Get off of me."

"Apologize."

"No. My house. My rules."

She tightened her grip. "Now."

Stars started dancing in front of him and his vision turned

blurry, but all he could focus on was the scent of her skin. She was nearly choking him and he found it a turn on. Had to be the lack of oxygen to his brain. "I could smash you like a bug," he warned her.

"But you won't." She brought her lips close to his ear and whispered, "Why don't you like me being nice to you?"

It wasn't a question he could answer.

Instead, he surprised her with a jab to the side, which loosed her grip, allowing him to flip her on the ground where she landed flat on her back.

She stared up at him stunned.

He didn't move. Horrified by what he'd done. Had he hurt her? He was bigger and stronger; perhaps he'd gone too far? He'd only meant to...

The unexpected sound of her laughter eased his fears and oddly lifted his heart. It was as surprising and lovely as seeing a rainbow reflected in a puddle.

"That maneuver was so good," she said, her brown gaze bright with amusement, awe and a little hero worship. "I didn't expect that." She rose to her feet with a slight wince. "Death-Hunter," she mumbled.

"What?"

"Never mind." She returned to the sink.

Bryant stared stunned at her bold defiance. "You must be joking."

Cat casually pulled on the gloves. "I promise I won't wash dishes again but I have to finish this. I'm almost done. Cross my heart."

Bryant took a menacing step forward. "What is wrong with you?"

Cat held up a handful of suds in a threatening manner.

He sniffed. "You think that can stop me?"

"A minor delay."

"You're—"

She moved her shoulders and wiggled her body like a devious little kid, delighting in mischief. "I know." Before he could reply she disarmed him by saying, "So when is your father moving in?"

"Moving in?"

"Yes, isn't that why you did all those renovations?"

No one else had guessed that. It had been an idea he'd been thinking of but never voiced.

"I did those for other reasons. He's comfortable where he is."

"I think he'd be happiest with you."

"Why would you think that?"

She shrugged. "Your relationship with your father is something special. You're not only father son but also friends. That's rare. Trust me. I couldn't imagine being friends with my parents." She shivered at the thought. "But you're different." She tossed a glance over her shoulder like a parent offering a child a life lesson. "There's nothing new with multi-generational living, you know. It might be considered a new trend in the US but we both know it's tradition elsewhere."

Bryant sighed, knowing the truth of her words but finding it hard to believe it. He could imagine the conversations. *You live with your father? No my father lives with me. For how long? It's permanent. That must be hard for you. Actually we get along great. You're so brave.* "It's not that simple. I—"

"There's nothing wrong with your father living with you," Cat said, making no allowance for his doubts. "Your house is big enough and he's such a gentleman he won't get under your feet. Whoever you plan to share your life with will understand that. And if you have kids, they'll adore him. He's so charming how could they help themselves?"

Why did she make the idea sound so...tempting? "Dad's worried he'd limit my options."

"He'll weed out the bad ones. And the jealous ones."

"Jealous ones?"

She turned to face him and wiggled her eyebrows. "The ones who want you all to themselves, he'd prove a threat." She turned back to the sink. "You don't want that. They'd want you to give up your art or your father and they're not worth it. Besides, whether he lives with you or not, you're a packaged deal. The woman in your life will have to accept that he's very important to you and you're both very close."

He folded his arms and frowned. Why did it have to be her? He'd always felt a little guilty about how close he was to his father even before the incident. And after...

Bryant rubbed his forehead as if to ease to pain of the memory.

They'd gone through so much (there had been plenty of rocky times, but his father continued to improve with the right diet, routine, medication and care) and she was one of the few to not see their relationship as a dependency, but as a genuine friendship.

It was as if she could see through into his heart, his soul. The ribbons of memories that tied him to his father: That Bryant took refuge in their weekly chats, their laughter filled lunches, the quiet walks, where they said nothing and just enjoyed each other's company.

She was giving him permission to be himself.

Isn't she the little girl who saved us? His father's words echoed in his mind.

Bryant felt his heart shift again just as the oven timer went off.

Cat's words had been unexpectedly wise and kind and understanding. She continued to be a mystery to him, but at least now he'd cracked the code to her cooking.

22

———

Except he hadn't.

Bryant and Cat sat at the dining table in silence after they'd both taken a bite of his first attempt.

It was serviceable, but nothing like they'd expected.

Bryant took a taste of her attempt, the one he'd carefully followed, and then he sampled his again and grimaced. The difference was so marked it stunned him.

"I guess I'm not as good a teacher as I thought," Cat said with regret.

"I don't think I was paying close enough attention," Bryant countered.

They shared a look.

"I'll make you another batch," Cat said at the same time Bryant said, "Show me again."

She laughed. "You trust me to teach you?"

"I missed something. It wasn't you."

She hesitated. "Are you sure?"

He set his fork down. "Yes."

UNFORTUNATELY, when Cat returned for a second attempt, it wasn't much better.

Bryant tossed his fork down and swore.

He still couldn't get the flavor right.

"Maybe I'm too much of a distraction," Cat said trying to lighten the mood. "You like cooking alone and having me in your kitchen—"

"It's not you. I'm going to get this. One more time."

But Cat's schedule was too busy so she told him she'd let him know when she was free again.

She didn't tell him she was busy because she had a date with his father.

MR. MEADOWS HAD CALLED her and made an odd request.

"I need to buy some cloth and I was told you could help me."

He didn't tell her much more than that. One Friday afternoon, she picked him up from his apartment and took him to two shops he'd written down.

The first shop, full of fine cloth and haughty clerks from South Asia, made it clear that she and Mr. Meadows didn't belong, a trip to another shop started by an East African woman wasn't much better. Clearly having an older man and an unattractive woman weren't the kind of clientele their shop wanted.

"Those bitches," Vanessa said, when Cat told her about the unsuccessful trips. They walked around World Foods where Cat was doing her shopping and Vanessa had joined her on her break from the wine store.

"It's okay," Cat said, cheered by her friend's anger on her behalf. "I should have known better."

"Why didn't you just take him to your parents' shop?"

"I didn't want questions, but I might have no other choice. He's being a bit cagey as to what he wants. But he keeps asking my opinion and holding up the cloth against me as if to see how it would look." She liked being with him. He had a way of making her feel seen.

"Do you think he has a woman?"

Cat laughed. "I don't know, but if he did, it wouldn't make sense for him to use me as a guide."

"You're not that bad."

"Doesn't matter. He asks me the oddest questions like what's your favorite season, what spice do I like. I don't know if he's just trying to make conversation or not."

"He sounds interesting."

"He is. I really like him and wish he'd trust me a little more. I'm not sure what he's up to and I don't want to say anything to Bryant and worry him in case it's innocent. But you're right. I'll take him to our store when I know someone who won't report to my parents isn't on duty."

That day arrived only three days later.

When they entered her parent's shop Mr. Meadows smiled and sighed, pleased.

"Yes, this is good."

He took his time and she let him, answering whatever question he had. When he made his final selection, he chose striking complimentary colors of red, orange and yellow.

"Someone will be very lucky," Cat said as the clerk rang up his purchases.

A secretive smile touched his lips. "It's only the beginning."

23

———

HE WAS ALMOST on top of her.

Not that he noticed. Bryant was so intent on learning Cat's cooking technique he'd forgotten to keep his distance, which was usually enough space for a row of semi-trucks to drive through.

However, with each visit, the distance seemed to close.

Meter by meter.

Inch by inch.

Until today when he stood so close behind her that Cat could feel his heat. Hear him breathing as he studied her every move.

She cleared her throat. "Wouldn't you be more comfortable—"

He reached past her and pointed. "I see how you mix that, I hadn't noticed before."

He might have noticed that but he *didn't* seem to notice how his bare arm brushed hers, not once or even twice but four times as he motioned to other items in front of them. He was so focused on the task she probably didn't even exist to him.

It was mildly irritating. She was used to being invisible but not this invisible.

But at least he wasn't looking at her as if she was gum he'd pulled off his shoe. He actually welcomed her into the kitchen and didn't mind when she cleaned up.

Over nearly two months, she had grown used to Bryant's amusing quirks. Not only did he sometimes talk to himself about random things when he was cooking he also did a running commentary like a voice over actor on what he observed saying things such as "Right and then she..." or "Oh she didn't put too much..." while he worked, which Cat found amusing because he seemed unaware of the habit.

She also made sure not to interrupt him with advice or instructions since it seemed he did best visually, watching her and talking to himself rather than hearing each step before he tried it on his own.

He accepted correction and she tried to give it using the distance she'd grown used to but he would motion her forward and say 'Show me' which she did before she took a hasty step back.

But recently he gave her no room to step back, as if he wanted her right up against him, which was impossible.

Strange how small the large kitchen could feel at times.

They put their latest attempt in the oven.

"I lied," she admitted.

"About what?"

"I wasn't able to find things in your kitchen because I know how you think. It's because you put things were I thought they'd go."

"Hmm."

"The rest were lucky guesses."

"Hmm."

"Just thought you should know."

"Why?"

She shrugged. "Because in case this doesn't work out—"

"We're going to get it."

Funny how he'd used the term 'we' it must have been unintentional but it still felt right. They did feel like a team trying to crack a code. She wanted him to get it right. Didn't particularly like him, still saw him as a fraud, but still wanted to see him succeed.

She headed for the kitchen exit, which had become her habit, then stopped.

She slowly turned. "Perhaps I should stay."

Bryant stared at her curious. "Think that will give me better luck?"

"Something like that."

He rubbed the back of his neck, considering the suggestion. "I've taken up a lot of your time already."

"And aside from cooking we have nothing in common."

"True."

"I like horror and thrillers and you don't."

He nodded.

"So we couldn't watch anything. And our musical tastes—"

"Do you still play the violin?"

Her eyes widened in surprise. "You remember that?"

"It's hardly something I'd forget," he said annoyed. "Do you still play?"

"Sometimes."

"Then bring it next time."

She grinned. "The reason I'm staying is because I'm hoping there won't be a next time."

"But in case there is...consider it."

"I will. Do you play an instrument?"

Bryant stared at her for a long moment before he said, "Come on."

He led her to his studio, which also functioned as an office. Cat entered the room with reverence taking in the color infused space—navy blue walls with aluminum shelving, hosting a rainbow display of books. A large ergonomic chair sat behind an enormous traditional rosewood desk. He touched a button and multiple monitors came to life as did the RGB backlit keyboard in a pop of purple and green.

On one screen she saw a textile design; on another a 3D concept of a lamp with one of his company's signature looks.

"This is how I make music," he said, also making his tablet come to life.

She stepped closer and peered down at his tablet, which had an image of a cute, cuddly looking...something. "Is this a mouse or a hamster or a gerbil?"

For a moment he looked shy.

"What?"

"I actually don't know yet," he said. "I've been fooling around with this character. I don't even know what it's for."

She sat in his chair then spun around to face him. "Well, I like it, so you'll have to figure out something." She smiled up at him.

Bryant gazed back at her looking a little ill.

"Are you okay?"

"I'm fine," he said in a clipped voice that told her he meant the opposite.

Cat realized her mistake. She'd made herself too comfortable in his sacred space. It had been hard enough to let him feel comfortable with her in the kitchen let alone a place like this. She jumped out of the chair. "Well, I think I've got some errands to—"

"Where are you going?" Bryant asked watching her dash out of the room.

"I just told you."

"Why are you running?"

"I'm not running," she said slowing down her pace. "I just want to get something done before I have to get back here."

"What just happened?"

Cat sighed. "It's okay. I know you made a mistake."

"A mistake?"

"And I did too."

He frowned. "What are you talking about?"

"You didn't mean to show me your studio."

He shook his head. "Yes, I did. I—"

"Maybe at first," she said, returning to the kitchen, "but then you regretted it. I'm sorry I sat in your chair. I wasn't thinking."

He released a sigh of frustration. "It wasn't the chair. It was what you said—"

"It wasn't my place. Again, I'm sorry."

He took a step forward and said in a soft voice, "Cat—"

She took a step back and waved him away. "Let's pretend it didn't happen."

He swore. "Cat—"

She began to talk quickly, almost frantically, wanting to say *Please don't explain, please don't explain. It'll hurt too much. I like you. I wish you liked me too.* "It's okay. I know we're not friends." She nervously licked her lips. "So I'll give you some space and—"

His gazed dipped to her mouth before returning to her eyes. "You don't have to do that."

"Yes, I do," she said, wondering why his quick glance made

her lips feel as if they were burning. She swallowed. "I know how you feel about me."

He sniffed and said in the grim tone of a condemned man, "I don't think you do."

"I saw the look on your face."

He glanced away and that was all the proof she needed. He still didn't like her, no matter how much she tried. "Better go," she said in a bright voice, determined not to reveal how much he'd hurt her. She turned. "See you in forty minutes. Don't forget to disinfect your chair." She'd meant it as a joke, but Bryant didn't take it as one.

He grabbed her wrist and spun her around with such force she bounced off his chest. The contact made all her senses come alive—the scent of his skin, the firm muscles, she wanted more. He quickly released her, rubbing his hands as if trying to rid himself of something disgusting.

Cat stared at his inscrutable expression, wide-eyed. "What was that about? Want to flip me over your shoulder again? Maybe toss me out the window?"

He didn't crack a smile. She realized he never smiled at her. She never got the benefit of the Bryant charm. Instead he was grimly resolute. His shook his head. "I don't regret it."

She blinked amazed. "Tossing me to the ground?"

"No," he said in a low, velvet tone. "Showing you my—" His phone rang. He swore.

She backed away. "You'd better get that," she said relieved by the chance to escape.

For a breath of a moment, Bryant looked as if he wasn't going to let her go. She felt the intense heat of his gaze, the power of his intention. As if he challenged her to take one more step and see if she could escape him.

Because he planned to make her stay.

But of course she had to have imagined that look, because it was quickly gone, like a mirage.

He released her from the snare of his gaze and answered the phone.

Cat left the kitchen, her face flushed, her heart racing. She wasn't sure what had just happened between them, but something had changed.

24

———

Bryant hated unfinished business.

He ended his phone call with Gareth and sagged against his kitchen counter.

Things hadn't ended well with Cat and he'd need to address it, but didn't know how. He'd have to think of something before she returned.

The little witch's power continued to grow; she enchanted him in surprising and endearing ways. He'd been amused by the reverence in which she'd entered his studio, the offhanded compliments and appreciation of his work.

But then she cast a spell that was nearly his undoing—she'd made him jealous of his favorite chair, forcing him to imagine the feel of her ripe little behind rubbing against him, soon she was naked and he imagined the warmth of her bared back pressed against his chest. Then she was facing him, her legs wrapped around him, her hot mouth covering his...

And it wasn't much better when he'd raced her to the kitchen.

It was the first time he'd seen her that vulnerable in spite of her big talk. Regrettably it only made him want her more. Watching how she nervously moistened her lips, the uncertainty in her gaze, tiny flame of desire burning there.

A flame he wanted to fan into a fire, like a predator aroused by fear. Except he didn't want her to fear him, he wanted her to crave his touch. To crave much more.

But grabbing her had been a reckless and dangerous move, he'd have to make up for that mistake and tread carefully.

The doorbell chimed and Bryant pushed himself from the counter as well as burying his thoughts. He'd been expecting visitors. Gareth had called to tell him he was minutes away from dropping his father off but wondered if Bryant had time to talk because he wanted to share something that was worrying him.

Minutes later, his father was happy upstairs in his room while Bryant and Gareth sat in the living room.

Gareth sat on the edge of the sofa as if terrified his clothes would stain the expensive fabric. He sipped the bottle of soda with ill-ease, as if Bryant had handed him a champagne glass. He treated the crackers and cheese spread with the same care, as if he'd been served caviar. He appeared so uncomfortable, Bryant considered talking him outside to the back patio. But before he could make that suggestion, Gareth said, "He's seeing a woman."

His first instinct was to ask, Who's seeing a woman, because he didn't want to believe his father could be taken again.

He took a deep breath. "Go on."

"She's young."

"How young?"

"Real young. I mean she might even be younger than me. A teenager, perhaps."

Bryant swore and gripped his fist wondering how the woman could have targeted his dad. "And?"

"They eat together and go to cloth shops."

Bryant paused not sure he'd heard correctly. "Cloth shops?"

He took another sip of his soda then carefully set it down on the coaster with a slightly trembling hand. "Yeah, you know where people buy fabric and stuff."

What the hell did this mean? What kind of scam was this young woman running? Could it be something romantic again? "Has he mentioned her to you?"

"No, that's what got me worried because he usually talks about everything. I checked and there aren't any sewing classes at the moment at the rec center or online. So I don't know what's going on."

Yes, his father would tell you what a store clerk he'd met on his grocery trip was wearing. If his father was keeping secrets, that was a bad sign.

Who was this 'young woman'? What could she be after?

"I don't think they're a couple or anything though."

Bryant felt some tension ebb, but not by much. He knew it could still be a scam. "Why not?"

Gareth suddenly looked embarrassed. "I didn't get the... you know, uh feel. It didn't seem um...you know."

"No," Bryant said, his patience thinning. "I don't know. Just say it."

"It didn't look like she hit the sock puppet."

Bryant stared at him blank. "I have no idea what that means."

Gareth muttered something in Spanish then said, "You know...like they had sex. Or-or wanted to. And it wasn't romantic. You know flirty like. They didn't touch each other like that. Plus she's not uh...I mean your dad's a good looking man. If he wanted a younger woman I don't think she'd be what he'd choose."

That sounded really mysterious. Even if this new relationship wasn't romantic, the woman (teenager?) could use him in another way.

"I didn't take any pictures," Gareth continued. "I'm sorry, I was just following like you told me to. But next time I can..." His words fell away and his eyes grew wide. He ran to the window.

Bryant jumped to his feet alarmed. "What is it?"

Gareth pointed. "T-that's her."

Bryant followed him to the window and saw Cat closing the trunk of her car, she'd returned earlier than he'd expected.

"Are you sure?"

Gareth nodded quickly. "Yeah, yeah. Positive." He turned to him. "Do you think he invited her here? What should we do? Do you want me to talk to her?"

"No. It's okay. I know her."

"You do?"

"Yes."

Well, that was a relief. At least his father hadn't found a stranger, but what was Cat doing taking his father around to fabric shops?

Bryant walked to the door and opened just as Cat was trying to hook a bag on the door handle. She missed and the bag fell to the ground.

25

SHE SWORE and quickly picked it up. "I hope they're not broken."

"What are you doing?"

"I was leaving a peace offering," she said, taking a box of shortbread cookies out of the bag. She lifted it to her ear and gently shook it. "Hopefully only a few are broken. They'll still taste good." She held out the box to him.

He stared at the box and shook his head. "I don't need a peace offering." He opened the door wider. "Come in."

"No, it's still early and—"

He snatched the box of shortbread cookies from her, opened it and shoved two cookies in his mouth. He chewed slowly while watching her, amused by her confusion before he swallowed and said, "I've accepted your peace offering. Now come in. I have a few things I need to ask you." He turned and walked to the living room, expecting her to follow.

Once they reached the living room, Bryant placed the box of cookies on the coffee table then motioned to the young man standing by the sofa.

"Cat, this is Gareth Mendez. Gareth, Cat Kayode."

She smiled at him. "Hello."

Gareth didn't reply. He stared—open mouthed. Like a kid who'd seen his first giraffe up close, completely fixated.

Bryant knew the kid was awkward, and Cat's slim build, large box braids and plain face took some getting used to, but gawking at her was rude.

Bryant walked over and nudged him. "What's wrong with you?"

"It's her."

"We've already established that."

Gareth shook his head. "No, not that." He crept close to Cat as if approaching something mystical.

"I'm right. It's you," he whispered. "You're Wicked Willa."

Bryant frowned. "Wicked what?"

Cat's smile grew. "I'm surprised you can recognize me without makeup."

"Wicked Willa," Gareth repeated in awe.

Cat laughed. "When I'm out of costume, I'm just Cat." She placed a hand over her heart and bowed her head. "A pleasure to meet you."

Gareth bounced up and down on his toes. "Am I dreaming? I never thought I'd meet you."

Bryant stared at the pair confused. "What is going on?"

Gareth pointed at him. "He doesn't know?"

Cat shrugged, nonplussed. "He wouldn't, it's not his thing."

"*He* is standing right here," Bryant said.

Neither took notice.

"How can he not know?" Gareth's eyes widened and he covered his mouth then let his hands fall and said, "Shit, was it supposed to be a secret? Is he your man, was he not supposed to know? Did I fu—"

"No, no it's okay," Cat quickly assured him. "You did nothing wrong. I'm still shocked you recognized me. People usually don't."

"You've got this way you walk and...It was such a wild show. I wasn't going to even go but a friend of mine convinced me and I damn...what a night."

Bryant approached them in a manner that made it impossible to ignore him. In a quiet voice he said, "What is going on?"

Gareth took out his phone then showed him a picture of two women dressed up with enough makeup to make an eighties rock star jealous, each holding musical instruments. Bryant spotted Cat and her violin right away.

He stared stunned.

"It's a side hobby," Cat said.

Bryant sent her an accusatory look. "You said you only played 'sometimes'."

"Which is true. It's just *sometimes* I play on stage. My family doesn't know. I always tell them I have a late course or something."

"She doesn't just play," Gareth said, "she messes with your mind. It can be scary as hell too. That video you did in the abandoned building, freaked me out."

Bryant couldn't understand why Gareth made that sound like a good thing.

"I'm glad," Cat said. "My friend's brother creates the films."

"And I remember the Halloween show last year. Every time I closed my eyes I heard that piercing violin and thought the Chainsaw man was coming to get me."

Cat laughed. "Thanks, Gareth. We were very pleased with that."

He suddenly looked sheepish. "Actually, my name's really Gary, but Mr. Meadows thought it was short for Gareth and I didn't feel like saying anything."

"I think he's right. Gareth suits you so if you don't mind us calling you that—"

"Nah, I don't mind. I like how he says it. Speaking of which, how did you make the Chainsaw man so terrifying when he didn't say anything?"

"That's a secret."

"What are you talking about?" Bryant asked.

"Their shows. I remember that movie screening," Gareth explained, "the really weird one that mixed old film footage of these gigantic flesh eating insects with current images, and it should have been stupid, you know, but they added their own music to it with some effects and...boom! The lights, the sounds, the screams."

It sounded like a nightmare to Bryant but Gareth looked so amazed he felt a little jealous he'd known something about Cat Bryant never had.

"When's your next show?" Gareth asked, checking his phone to find their website.

"We've been on hiatus but we are working on something again for this October."

Gareth danced on the tips of his toes again with excitement. "Can't wait." He then asked her about a movie (or was it a game? he wasn't quite sure) Bryant had never heard of and for a moment he felt the age difference between them.

Eight years felt like eighty. Gareth was closer in age to Cat than he was. Not that it should matter, right?

He could dismiss the age, but he and Cat were different in

so many other ways. He didn't like loud music or horror shows, he despised Halloween.

Soon Cat and Gareth started talking in a language he couldn't understand about scream levels, jump scares and basement versus deserted city settings.

Bryant watched them feeling like the awkward thirteen year old immigrant from England who felt out of step with everything, unlike his older brother who seemed to be the master of adapting. Like their mother, who'd come to the US to study medicine, his brother excelled in academics, graduating high school early and eventually becoming an astrophysicist. Leaving their mother to despair why Bryant wasted his time on drawing instead of studying. He'd been an average student who'd learned to use dry humor, a quick smile and his ability to draw to put people at ease and hide his own anxieties.

Those anxieties renewed themselves now as he watched the easy manner in which Cat and Gareth interacted. He'd never be able to manage that with her. He'd gotten a box of broken cookies as a peace offering.

He left them and went upstairs to confront his father about buying cloth with Cat. Then stopped halfway up the stairs. If he asked him about the cloth his father might ask him how he knew and he didn't want to admit Gareth's role nor did he want to lie. It'd be better to ask Cat. Bryant turned and started towards the living room, but the sound of Cat and Gareth's laughter set his teeth on edge.

He swore and marched into the kitchen willing the oven timer to go off, but there was too much time left.

He increased the heat to make it cook faster, which he never did. He knew that the increased temperature could ruin his efforts and he didn't care. Part of him hoped it did.

He felt unmoored, restless and jealous. But more than that,

he felt foolish for desiring someone clearly wrong for him and he was wrong for her.

By the time the oven timer went off and Gareth said his goodbyes, the chicken they pulled out of the oven looked as appetizing as cooked cardboard.

And tasted like seasoned rubber.

"I don't know what happened," Cat said, setting down her fork, staring at the food confused.

Bryant sat back in his chair. "Guess we'll just have to try again."

She folded her arms and sent him a suspicious look. "What did you do?"

He looked back bored. He'd admit to nothing.

She narrowed her eyes. "I'd wondered why you disappeared when I was talking to Gareth."

She'd noticed? He felt a petty delight in that.

"I know Gareth and I got carried away. We didn't mean to make you feel left out," she said in an indulgent tone, as if she were soothing a petulant child.

"It's fine." He cleared his throat. "You two have a lot in common."

She looked at him for a long moment until he said, "What?"

"I know this is a lot to ask." She bit her lip. "And after you rejected my peace offering—"

His brows shot up. "I ate it, didn't I?"

"And then you destroyed our experiment."

He blinked. Nope, he still wouldn't deny or admit a thing. "What do you want?"

"I could use your artistic eye. I want a new look for our next show. If you had some ideas..."

"If you want to terrify people just go as you are."

Cat stood and came around the table.

He watched her with rising dread and curiosity.

Before he could ask her what she was doing, she bent down and licked his cheek.

It wasn't quick, like the flicker of a snake's tongue; it was slow, deliberate, hot.

Bryant jumped up, his hand to his face. "Bloody hell! What was that?"

She flashed a mischievous grin. "Punishment. Bet you'll jump in the shower the moment I leave."

26

———————

HER WORDS PROVED PROPHETIC.

He did jump in the shower, but not for the reason she thought.

He couldn't shower long enough to cool down his aching desire; the sensual memory of her wet tongue, sliding against his skin.

It was torture. Sweet torture.

He became more determined than ever to get her to feel the same, to make her see him in another light.

He didn't care how different they were, how little they had in common, until he was able to quench this thirst, this simmering fire, he could not rest.

So much so his friend noticed.

"The Old Woman's been asking about you," Keeden said one afternoon as they sat on Keeden's patio, and watched a light summer drizzle slowly wash away the chalk art image of colorful, swirling shapes they'd quickly drawn on the stone path in the garden.

After a business meeting, they liked to relax by using

cheap chalk and creating spontaneous original art.

Bryant was glad to see his friend freely creating again; the accident had shaken Keeden's confidence and even after his cast had been removed, his friend worried that his abilities might have left him. But with Maya's help, Keeden had regained his confidence in not only his art but himself and the bold dramatic image he'd sketched proved he had nothing to worry about.

Usually, at the end of a chalk drawing session, they'd either wash it away with a hose or pressure washer. This time the rain was helping them out, making the image appear as if it were moving as colors shifted and melded and slowly disappeared.

They reminded him of his thoughts, which he couldn't seem to pin down.

Bryant took a sip of his limeaid with a slight grimace. Between worrying about his Dad and cooking with Cat he hadn't made time for fourteen year old Lena as he used to.

"I'll call her."

"Is everything okay with Uncle?" Keeden asked using an affectionate and respectful term for Bryant's father. Since they were teenagers, Keeden had never called Bryant's father Mr. Meadows.

"Yes, why?"

"You seem preoccupied. What's going on?"

Bryant tapped his finger against the cool glass. "I'm not sure," he admitted. "My Dad's been shopping with Cat."

Keeden paused with his glass halfway to his mouth. "Did you just say Cat?"

Bryant nodded.

Keeden slowly set his glass down. "That's strange. What are they buying?"

"That's where it gets even stranger. They're buying cloth."

"For what?"

Bryant shrugged. "Haven't asked him yet. I'm waiting to see what happens."

"Or you could ask him. I wouldn't worry about it. You may hate her but she's not as awful as you think. I'm sure it's harmless."

"Hmm."

Keeden tossed one of his long braids over his shoulder, leaned forward and said, "Now tell me what's really bothering you."

"I just did."

Keeden sat back and folded his arms. "Two months before your wedding."

Bryant swore, feeling the acute pain of that unhappy memory. "You don't have to bring that up."

His friend continued without remorse. "I caught you sitting alone in our shared DC studio looking like a grave robber facing execution. You were tormented. You have that same expression now. You're conflicted. Tell me what's going on."

He couldn't. He didn't know what to say, he didn't even know how to deal with his feelings let alone express them in words.

His cancelled engagement somehow felt even easier than now. Even though he'd hurt a lot of people, he knew he couldn't be the husband his former fiancée expected him to be, that he'd been pretending with her when she deserved someone real.

Fortunately, she soon found someone else and Bryant was relieved of the guilt, though he'd become more careful in the present, making sure to keep his relationships light and easy.

He didn't know how to have a relationship with someone other than Keeden or his father, when he wasn't pretending.

And Cat wasn't someone to toy with.

And they had little in common.

But he didn't care.

Unless...

But he had to give his friend something or Keeden would keep prying so Bryant decided to tell him something else. He told him about meeting and hiring Gareth and added, "I'm spying on him and I'm not sure that's right. That's how I found out he's been shopping with Cat."

"Why the need to spy?"

"You know what happened."

"Yeah, but don't you think this is an extreme response? It happened years ago. I can have Maya talk to Cat if this really bothers you."

"No, it's okay."

He hated keeping things from his friend but knew it wasn't safe to tell him the truth. First, he probably wouldn't believe him, then he'd warn him against Cat because if things went sour with Cat it could impact his relationship with Maya, the family dynamics were already fractured with the mother. And then he might tell him a truth Bryant didn't want to hear—that he wasn't the right man for Cat. That he had too much baggage. That he didn't know how to be real.

"Careful there," Keeden warned him.

"Don't worry I am," Bryant said, surprised his friend had managed to read his thoughts.

"I think you should stop it now if it's bothering you this much."

"I know I should, but I can't." He sighed, relieved to admit the truth. "It's as if Cat brings out the best and worst in me."

He took a sip of his drink then noticed his friend sending him a long, measured look.

"What?"

Keeden shook his head. "I wasn't talking about Cat."

Bryant swallowed, his mouth suddenly dry. "You weren't?"

"No. Why would I? I know how much you can't stand the woman. Why would I bring her up?"

"I don't know," Bryant said feeling trapped. "Because we were talking about my dad and her shopping trips with him."

Keeden narrowed his eyes. "I see."

Bryant glanced down at the ice melting in his glass, hoping he hadn't given too much away. "W-who were you talking about?"

"The kid you hired." Keeden rubbed his forehead. "Look. I know you want to paint Cat as the villain in this," he smiled, "and we both know she can make a great villain. But I don't think she is. If you want, I can talk to her—"

Bryant lifted his gaze. "No. I said I'll handle it."

"Promise me you won't accuse her of anything. Listen to what she has to say. Don't let your dislike cloud your judgment."

His friend had no idea how much Bryant's feelings for Cat had changed and he couldn't tell him. Not yet. "I will. Don't worry."

Bryant shifted his gaze to the chalk drawing that the drizzle had rendered a mere shadow of its former self.

And as he listened to the steady, soft rainfall hit the ground, inhaled the fragrance of the damp flowers and watched as droplets caused the image to completely fade away, a strategy began to form in his mind.

He'd seduce Cat like the rain: subtly, softly and patiently.

27

Cat considered not going back.

After the incident with the chair in Bryant's studio and then knowing, he deliberately ruined the food and denied it (!), she felt uneasy with him.

That had never happened before.

For two days she anticipated a phone call or text.

She was certain he'd call her to cancel on his own. His expression when she'd licked him had been worth the effort.

But what surprised her was that for a moment, he didn't look disgusted or outraged, he looked aroused. She almost wanted to lick him again.

Her imagination truly was a dangerous thing.

It was that wild imagination that let another day pass before she texted him a date and time when she was free. She deleted and retyped the message three times before she eventually hit Send.

And regretted it.

What if Bryant said, Don't bother. Or said he was busy and then never got back to her or...

She put her phone away and opened her laptop.

She tried to focus on the movie clip Vanessa's brother had sent her. But as the minutes ticked by, and her text received no reply, Cat's thoughts grew more and more grim. Perhaps she'd really pushed him too far.

Nearly twenty minutes later her phone alerted her to a text.

She opened it and noticed it wasn't a text but an image.

On a round blue plate Bryant had used an orange slice, sliced apples, mandarin slices, green grapes, pretzel sticks and raisins to depict an image of a bird flying off a green meadow towards a sun, with the raisins spelling the letters OK. It was touching and funny and beautiful. She thought of her rudimentary image of the words OK spelled out with simple fruit. This was art.

She texted him. *Show off*

Impressed?

Which part of the picture represents your ego? The sun or the sky?

Both

<image of cat laughing>

Cat put down her phone relieved Bryant had truly forgiven her.

Unfortunately, after giving feedback on the movie clip, Cat found herself gazing at the fruit art and feeling more than relief.

Longing. She couldn't stop thinking about him. She no longer saw him as a fraud. Or imagined him as Death-Hunter. She thought of the man who talked to himself when he was in the kitchen, the one who loved cooking as much as she did. She thought of how the light seemed to know just where to strike his face to make his eyes sparkle, to soften the hard edge of his mouth and soften his lips.

Lips that never smiled for her.

Cat buried her face in her pillow. It was hopeless! How stupid to think he ever would smile at her like he did everyone else.

She never imagined she'd end up with a crush on him like Maya once had.

At least Maya was cute and artistic. Cat never desired to be cute and had the artistic ability of a hamster. She wasn't romantic and would rather jump off a cliff than talk about emotions.

But it didn't stop her from liking him more than she should.

Cat sat up and slapped her cheek. The stinging pain helped put her thoughts back in order.

Once Bryant could replicate her secret he wouldn't need her anymore.

The most she could hope for was to be acquaintances.

Maybe...with a little effort and time...they could be friends.

Somehow that thought depressed her more.

But she buried her pesky thoughts and feelings and arrived at Bryant's house ready to focus on cooking.

She rang the doorbell.

A stranger opened the door.

28

____

The stranger looked exactly like Bryant.

He had the same build, the same manners, but there was something different about the eyes.

Something that reminded her of the man she'd seen in Arizona.

There was a lazily lethal calm as he leaned against the doorframe. "You're early."

"I can wait in the car if you like."

"No," he said straightening, his movements reminding her of a puma. "I'm glad you're here."

She met his gaze, wondering if he was teasing her, and found herself captured by mesmerizing brown eyes.

Yes, this man was definitely a stranger. A man she didn't know whether to fight or flee, who walked along the shadows as neither babyface nor heel.

Neither hero nor villain.

One she couldn't pin down.

She glanced at her car and thought of the safety it would provide her. "Maybe I should—"

Bryant gently pulled her inside. "It's not like you to be indecisive."

"It's not like you to be—" Cat stopped and bit her lip. She couldn't admit that she found him confusing.

"What?" he said. He softly closed the door behind her, daring her to finish.

"So cocky."

He didn't smile, but he looked amused. "That's not what you were about to say, but I'll let it pass because I have something for you." He handed her a folded piece of paper. "Tell me what you think."

Cat held the rectangular paper by one of its corners and examined it. "I think you have great folding skills."

"Open it."

She did and gasped at the sight.

He'd sketched her face with a new makeup scheme for her onstage persona. It was good. Too good.

He'd honored her request in a way she never thought he would. She shook her head. "I could never look like this."

"Of course you can."

"I'd have to practice hours to make this work," she said. "I'm not this good with makeup. I'll pay you to buy the makeup for me, but only a professional would be able to—"

Bryant snatched the paper and crumbled it into a ball, ignoring her cry of outrage. "I'll sketch you something simpler then."

"No! Give it back."

"I can—"

She tried to pry his fist open. "No, I want this one."

"Why?"

"Because it's mine. Open your palm right now or I'll lick you again."

"Is that a promise?"

She blinked, startled. "What?"

He tossed the paper at her. "Never mind."

She caught it and mumbled, "What is wrong with him?" as she smoothed out the paper on her thigh. She shot him a glance. "Why did you do that?"

"It's just a sketch. I can do another one."

She wasn't listening. Instead she continued to smooth out the paper then held it in her hands and stared at it with a slight frown.

"What's wrong?"

"Some idiot crumbled up my picture."

Bryant sighed. "Look, I can draw you another one—exactly the same."

"And why did you fold the picture up in the first place? Was it so that it didn't seem important? "

"No, I folded it up because I liked seeing you open it."

She rested her hands on her hips.

He shrugged. "Okay, you're right. I didn't want to make it a big deal."

"Okay."

When she continued to stare at him Bryant finally said, "What?"

"I'm waiting. You said you can draw me another one that's exactly the same. I'm assuming it won't take long."

"No."

"Then I'll wait." She walked into the living room, sat down and pulled out her phone.

Bryant opened his mouth to argue but Cat waved her hand and said, "No picture, no cooking lesson."

Bryant merely nodded and headed for his studio.

The moment he was gone, Cat fell back against the sofa

and stared up at the ceiling. She didn't really need him to sketch another image. She needed distance.

Bryant wasn't acting like himself and neither was her heart. It wouldn't stop racing, her skin felt hot.

Is that a promise?

He'd responded to her threat as if he welcomed it. Wanted her. His deep voice and penetrating gaze almost willing her to try.

Had he misheard her threat?

Did he think she was bluffing?

Cat closed her eyes and took a deep breath.

What about the sketch? That had been a complete surprise.

It was one of the nicest things someone had ever done for her.

Bryant had done her a favor?

Sure, she'd asked him, but she hadn't expected the result to be so detailed and in full color.

And why had he made her look so...good? He could have made her look horrible, she knew her plain features weren't much to work with. But he'd done the opposite. He'd made her look amazing. If only she could find a way to make it work. He seemed confident she could.

She took some money out of her wallet and shoved it in her back jeans pocket. It wasn't a lot to give him to pick up some makeup for her, but it was a start. He'd helped her so much.

Maybe...he was starting to like her a little bit? And if he did...

Cat sat up and shook her head. She couldn't think about that right now. Once Bryant returned with the new sketch they'd head into the kitchen and this time she was determined they would succeed.

She looked at her phone and searched through her calendar.

It was a busy month and after missing picking up her father's dry cleaning her mother had gotten a little suspicious as to what Cat was really doing with her time. She had to make sure her other activities didn't get in the way. She almost didn't want to have to stop coming by Bryant's. It had become a habit she'd grown used to. She'd grown used to him and she'd miss him. She'd miss him even more now that he was actually being nice.

"What are you doing?" a deep voice said behind her.

Cat jumped as if a ghost had brushed past her. She looked over her shoulder and glared at Bryant. "When did you start sneaking up on people?"

He knelt down and rested his forearms on the back of the sofa. "I learned from a master," he said in an amused voice.

Cat leaned forward, wondering when he'd gotten comfortable being so close. In the kitchen he was focused on cooking, but here...his gaze seemed to be focused on her.

She cleared her throat, returned her attention to her phone and held out her hand, ready to receive her sketch.

What she didn't expect was the feel of warm lips pressed against her palm.

29

CAT SNATCHED her hand away and stared at him stunned. "What was that?"

"Payback," Bryant said, pleased by how much he'd rattled her. Before giving her a chance to recover, he came around the couch and distracted her by tossing the revised sketch on the seat beside her then picking up her phone from her lap where she'd dropped it in surprise.

He skimmed her digital calendar amazed by how many colors and letters filled almost every day. "What is that?"

"What does it look like?" she asked reaching for the phone. "Appointments and errands and such."

He gently pushed her away and continued to stare. Her calendar hardly had any white space. 'Mom' popped up a lot. He never imagined Cat's life would be so cluttered. He saw today's date and saw a strange symbol and initials DH and assumed it was how she'd categorized him. He wasn't sure he wanted to know what DH stood for but a sense of guilt came over him.

He handed her the phone, his mood sinking.

He realized he was just another obligation to her, something she'd squeezed in the middle of the day. He'd never considered that she had a life. Until now, there was never cause to see her as a person. He knew she worked in her family's businesses but never thought of how she spent the rest of her time. He'd never thought she'd have to come over so many times because he kept screwing up.

He quickly glanced at her. She did look a little tired today. He hadn't noticed before. Hadn't cared.

They went to the kitchen but Bryant didn't pay much attention as he prepped the items.

How many places did her mother need to go to? And when did Cat have time for herself? And why hadn't he even thought of how he'd forced her to come to see him?

He thought about the smashed jar. How angry she'd been at him for not even trying. How long had it taken her to make the mix? Why hadn't he even thought of that? And he'd been wasting her time because he couldn't—"

"It's okay," Cat said.

Bryant turned to her. "What?"

"I don't mind coming."

He paused. Was she a mind reader?

"You've been talking to yourself the entire time," she said, answering his silent question.

He swore. She giggled.

"I would have stopped you," she said, "but I liked hearing what you were thinking. It's not easy to guess."

He turned away and continued chopping.

"I wouldn't be here if I didn't have a reason. I like seeing you struggle."

She was teasing him and he knew it, but it didn't stop him from still being embarrassed for voicing his thoughts aloud. At least they weren't more personal, intimate thoughts. He had to gain better control.

"Do you ever say no?" he asked.

Cat laughed. "You say that as if I have a choice."

"Don't you?"

She considered his question for a moment before she said, "Sort of. When it comes to my mother, it's not so much a choice as a consequence. I choose the kinds of consequences I want to deal with. That's the best way of handling her. Most times saying yes is easier."

"Does your family know you've been coming here?"

"No way. They think I'm attending a class. Besides, it'd hurt my pride to share I'm revealing my secret to you of all people."

"You have me down as DH."

"Yes."

"What does that stand for?"

She hesitated then said, "Dedicated Homemaker."

He blinked then threw his head back and laughed. "No, it doesn't."

"You're right."

"But you're quick on your feet. So what's it really mean?"

She shook her head. "No way am I telling you that."

"Why not?"

"I bet you have me down as Demon Seed," she said with a smirk.

"Naw, I changed it."

"To what?"

Bryant waved his knife. "You first."

"Forget it. You wouldn't understand." She spun away. "Let's see if we can get closer to success."

30

He'd gotten it.

He couldn't believe it.

Cat smiled at him but Bryant couldn't smile back. It was strange how smiling usually came easily to him, but not with her. It didn't mean he wasn't happy. He was buoyant.

"Congratulations," she said, putting her fork down and clapping her hands. "A hard won victory."

He nodded.

She stood. "Now that you know my secret you must take it with you to your grave."

The thought struck him. She wasn't coming back. It was over. He wasn't ready yet. He needed more time.

"What about seafood?"

"It's not that much different."

"Show me."

Cat made a dismissive wave of her hand. "You don't need me to do that. We've gone over enough that you've acquired the technique. You've mastered this. The rest is up to you."

She was going to leave and he'd have no other reason to see her again. It could be months. He didn't want it to be months.

He rubbed his hands on his thighs searching his thoughts. "But I want..." He trailed off. He couldn't say it.

"Let's clean up the kitchen."

Minutes later the only evidence they'd been cooking was a warm oven, a wet sink and the scent of spices.

Cat took off her apron with a flourish. Her job was done.

She didn't know why Bryant didn't seem as happy as she'd expected him to be.

He stood at the counter, his hands flattened on it, his arms tense, like corded steel.

She crept up and slid her hand across the counter until it touched his. He didn't move away, he didn't flinch.

Instead he shifted his gaze to her face and looked at her in a way he never had before. He didn't look annoyed. He didn't look afraid.

Her heart froze.

If he wasn't annoyed or afraid of her anymore what did that mean? That had been her power over him—she'd been able to provoke him, to make him react. He was one of the few people who noticed her, saw her and felt something.

But if he'd become numb to her, then he'd treat her as everyone else did. She'd become invisible or worse—treated like a piece of furniture.

She shouldn't have helped him. She should have stopped when she'd had the chance.

Now he didn't need her or fear her and it was a devastating loss. She blinked back tears.

She looked down at his hand, unmoving, still touching hers, he'd never have allowed that before. She slowly lifted her gaze to his face, prepared to see him looking right through her or somewhere else.

But his gaze hadn't move from her face and wait...what was that look in his eyes? It wasn't fear, but an emotion that felt just as intense. She wasn't invisible to him. Far from it.

The look in his eyes reminded her of the stranger she'd met at the door. The one who frightened her a little, and intrigued her a lot.

What could this look mean? This dark, probing gaze?

Why did it elicit a delicious sweet terror within her?

Make her skin tingle, her lips burn, her heart pound?

Cat licked her lip. Swallowed.

It couldn't be desire, though? Could it?

"I should..." She let her words fade away as she watched him slowly shake his head. His gaze never leaving hers until she couldn't bear it anymore and looked down.

But when he didn't move or say anything she took a chance and glanced up again and saw he looked amused.

Amused?

She folded her arms, gathering courage. "What's so funny?"

"Did I say anything was funny?"

"It's the look on your face."

"And what is that look telling you?" he said just above a whisper.

"I don't know."

"Yes, you do."

"No, I don't. It's impossible."

"What is?"

She lowered her head. "Never mind. I really—"

Bryant lifted her chin. "I like you."

Cat opened her mouth then closed it.

His gaze dipped to her lips, his voice deepened. "Can I show you how much?"

Rendered speechless, she could only nod. Then shook her head. No, this had to be a joke. This had to be...

Heaven. Pure, sweet, heaven.

The delicious taste of his lips removed all doubt. She wrapped her arms around his neck, deepening the kiss. He made a sound—a growl, a groan, she didn't know—but it came from deep within him, a response that sent shivers through her.

They were followed by the sound of trumpets. It took her a moment to realize Bryant's cell phone was ringing.

He swore. "It's my dad. I've got to answer it."

"Okay," Cat said dazed, her lips still warm from his kiss. She took a step back, trying her best to collect herself and think rationally again. "I'll see you later."

"Second door on the left."

"What?"

My room, Bryant mouthed before he answered the phone and said in a bright voice, "Hi Dad." He grabbed her hand, when she still continued to stare at him motionless, and led her to the stairs. "No, no you haven't caught me at a bad time," he said to his father as he took her up the stairs. He gestured to a door. "You know I always have time for you." He held up his hand to Cat and mouthed, *Five minutes*, before he headed back downstairs and she couldn't hear the rest of his conversation.

His bedroom door stood partially ajar. Cat grabbed the door handle and pulled the door closed. She rested her head against it and shut her eyes, trying to stop her mind from spinning; her heart pounded so hard it almost hurt.

Never in a trillion years could she have imagined this. She

couldn't believe this was real. Just beyond this door was Bryant's bedroom, his bed and he wanted her in it.

The thought made her feel lightheaded and she feared she'd walked into his room and faint and he'd end up finding her on the floor.

Five minutes.

She didn't have time. He'd be back soon.

She took a deep breath. She slowly opened the door and felt as if she were crossing a threshold as she left the hallway.

31

The other side.

Those were the first thoughts that entered her mind when she walked into Bryant's bedroom. It seemed more contained and yet wilder than she'd expected it to be. He'd given his father the master suite and saved a pale imitation for himself. And pale was the best way to describe the room. From the eggshell white walls, the light grey furnishings, it held none of the dark tones he'd used in the kitchen.

It exposed a carefree, lighter side and yet it was messier than she'd thought it would be. She noticed a purple sweater tossed over the back of a chair, one striped sock on the ground, which made her wonder where the other could be, and then there was the bed.

Its unmade disarray seemed to make it loom larger than it actually was.

Cat walked over to the bed and stripped to her bra and panty and got under the soft, light beige sheets. His scent still clung to them. She wiggled out of her panty but paused when her thigh scraped another fabric. She reached down and pulled out a bra.

A sexy, black bra with geometric designs.

It was too small to be his, if he was into such a thing.

It definitely belonged to someone else.

How long ago had another woman been in this bed? Last night? Last week?

Who was she and what did she mean to him?

Cat expected Bryant to have had other partners. She'd even had one brief—boringly disappointing—encounter in college. After that, she'd had no time and little interest in having another one until now. But she wasn't sure willingness and enthusiasm would cover her lack of experience.

She couldn't compete with someone who wore a sexy, black bra with geometric designs. She wasn't sexy or romantic and never wanted to be. That was completely out of her league.

Cat thought of getting dressed again and leaving. She didn't want the memory of this woman overshadowing her. She didn't want him to think of her as a brief moment of pleasure when she wanted to mean more to him.

I like you. Can I show you how much?

Would he? Could she show him how much she liked him too? Should she hold back?

She heard his footsteps and thought about tossing the bra at him and making her escape, but realized she didn't want to. Even if being with him was a mistake, she wanted it. She quickly shoved the bra under the mattress just seconds before the door swung open.

And Death-Hunter entered the arena.

Majestic, bold, fierce.

She watched him toss off his shirt, his jeans and boxer

briefs, while his eyes captured and held hers, as he made his way to the bed.

This was a performance she planned to enjoy. She watched him slid on protection with growing anticipation. She was ready for this.

The moment Bryant kneeled on the bed, Cat knew she couldn't hold back.

And when he touched her, she didn't want to.

I like you.

He showed her without words, his body eloquent and clear, telling her all she needed to know, revealing his feelings in a way that shocked her. The depth of his feelings not only leaving her breathless, but gasping.

Tiny fissures of fear coursed through her, her body was so much smaller and weaker in comparison to his, her movements and responses seemed insufficient. She wished she was more substantial, had more for him to hold.

"Simmer," he said, a whispered word heavy with meaning. She'd said that to him once when he'd grown impatient with one of her instructions and handled the food roughly.

She reminded him why sometimes we put food on the stove to simmer, to remind him to cook food gently, with patience and care. But more than that, letting something simmer just below the boiling point, was a strategy of both control and letting go. Letting temperature and time and instinct rule, not rational thought. She wasn't meant to think, she was meant to simmer.

Yes, he was right. This was not a time for fear or hesitation.

She was exactly where she wanted to be and she wanted him to know that.

She made him inhale sharply when she tightened around

him, teased his nipples with her tongue, slid her fingers down his thigh, across his chest.

Her hand brushed against a raised scar and she felt as if she were reuniting with an old friend. She'd been there when he'd gotten this wound. She wondered if they'd ever talk about that day. She wouldn't be the first to mention it again. She doubted it held any good memories, although one day she'd tell him how he'd changed her life.

But not yet, not now.

Right now Death-Hunter was teaching her things she didn't know. That the taste of a lover's lips could be as delectable as marshmallow fudge, that a lover's scent could be more aromatic than fresh strawberry lemonade, that a lover's touch could make you forget yourself, forget your imperfections and remind you that they didn't matter.

Only the exultant wave of their passion and the declarations it made.

Eventually, they fell away, breathless and spent.

Still feeling heavy limbed, Cat lifted herself up first and touched his chest, ready for another round, but froze when she noticed the time on his side table.

"What is it?" Bryant asked, sensing her tension.

She jumped up and swore. "That can't be the time." She scrambled out of bed. "It's close to dinnertime. I'm going to be in so much trouble."

She pulled on her clothes.

Bryant leaned on his side and watched her dash around the room. "Tell them there was traffic."

"They'd find out the truth. Damn apps."

She patted her back jeans pocket. "Oh, before I forget. Thanks again for everything." She pulled out the dollar bills she'd stuffed there and tossed them at him.

Bryant shot up with the rage of a prodded bull. "What the —" He shoved the money off the bed, his eyes flashed with fire. "Is that what you think this was?"

Cat frowned, surprised by his outrage. "You don't think you deserve it?"

His voice cracked in surprise. "Deserve it?"

"Yes."

Bryant briefly shut his eyes before he walked to his closet and put on a robe. "Get out."

"What?"

He spun around, his voice a low warning. "If I have to repeat myself, I won't be nice."

"I don't understand why you're upset," Cat mumbled as she gathered the money from off the ground. "Oh, I get it. You don't like cash, right? I can send it to you electronically."

He narrowed his eyes. "If you're not out of here in three seconds—"

"Just tell me how much you need for the makeup and I'll give it to you."

Bryant stared at her blank. Blinked. Rubbed his forehead. Took a deep breath. Leaned against the closet door. "Cat?"

"Yes?"

"What. Are. You. Talking. About?"

"The makeup. I said you'd have to buy it for me, remember? The design you drew is so intricate I wouldn't know where to start and you already did me a favor by coming up with the design I don't expect you to pay for the supplies too."

He studied her then spoke slowly and carefully. "The money you just threw at me is for me to buy you makeup?"

"Yes."

Bryant slowly slid to the ground, hung his head and said, "Somebody save me from this woman."

"What did I do?"

He started to laugh.

Cat stared at him unsure. She liked the sound of his laughter but it also left her confused. One moment he's furious and the next he's laughing? "What's so funny?"

Bryant shook his head. "Only you'd toss money at a guy after sex and not realize it's an insult."

"An insult?"

Bryant got up, walked over to her and took the money from her hand. He quickly counted the total amount. "Eighty? If I charged by the hour, this would definitely be an insult."

Cat blinked. "By the hour? What are you talking about? Why would you char..." Her words fell away as she took in the scintillating peek of bare flesh underneath his robe, the money he held in his hand. Realization slowly dawned. "Ohhhh. Noooo."

"Ohhhh. Yesss," Bryant said mimicking her tone.

She stared at him devastated. "I'd never. I didn't mean—"

"I know." He placed the money in her palm and wrapped her fingers around it. "Now you'd better leave before I make you pay for that misunderstanding."

"I'm so sorry. Please don't—"

A well placed kissed stopped her words.

32

———————

AHHH YES...THIS. Bryant thought as Cat's fingers made their way up his chest. This is what it feels like.

Cat's fingers were better than he'd dreamed. She approached him as she approached cooking—assertive, confident, creative. She knew what she wanted from him, and like a skilled chef able to reveal the most subtle flavor in a food, she discovered his deepest, most guarded self. He couldn't hide. He could never hide from her.

He wasn't ready to let her go.

He drew back and said in a coaxing tone, "You don't have to go yet. I can have Keeden come up with an excuse for you."

She hesitated.

She *hesitated* responding to his suggestion.

That one action seared him like an iron rod. Because it wasn't the hesitation of someone who wanted to stay, but one who wanted to leave.

She cast a glance at the bed, the corners of her mouth briefly turning down, before she returned her gaze to his face and smiled. "I can't," she said and he heard a note of regret in her voice, but he didn't believe her.

Why had she looked at the bed? Why had she frowned? What was she holding back? He was a skilled lover and yet... He hadn't won her completely and he didn't know where he'd gone wrong. He'd given all of himself and still it wasn't enough.

He'd offered her more time with him, possibly an entire night, not only a couple hours, and she'd *hesitated*.

She wasn't ready to fully accept him.

Maybe, she wasn't supposed to. Maybe he'd expected too much. Perhaps he'd done better wearing the mask he'd worn with all his past lovers. Perhaps that's what Cat had wanted, a more carefree lover. One not so intense, raw, vulnerable.

He gathered the front of his robe in his fist, amazed that she still had the ability to make him feel small.

But now she even made him feel clingy and needy because he didn't want her to go and he wanted to see her again. One time with her hadn't satiated his desire. Once wouldn't be enough.

A new terror entered his mind, one he didn't want to think about. Thoughts about growing attached and the future. She'd already wielded a greater power over him than he should have let her.

If he was smart, he'd leave it at this.

"Tell me when you get the makeup and I'll come by and pick it up." She put on her shoes then opened the bedroom door.

Bryant sighed. The makeup. All she cared about was the makeup. She dashed down the stairs; he followed behind at a more leisurely pace. "I can just have it delivered to your house."

"No, then I'd have to explain it." She grabbed her things from the living room then returned to the foyer.

He leaned against the staircase railing, ready to see her leave so he could be left alone with his misery. "I can package it differently," he said in a bored tone. "It's not a big deal."

She didn't move, which seemed strange since only seconds before she seemed eager to leave. "But I wouldn't want you to go through the trouble."

Bryant walked over to the front door and opened it, hoping it would encourage her to start moving again. "It's no trouble."

"But..."

"But what?" he said in a sharp tone when she stared at him helpless.

Cat glanced at the stairs, at him, then she shook her head and turned to the door.

She was halfway out the door, with Bryant prepared to close the door behind her, when she abruptly turned to him and said in a rush, "I wanted an excuse to come by and see you."

"An excuse?"

She nodded. "Without the cooking sessions, I don't have a reason to come over."

Damn. Was she really this clueless? She truly had no idea how much she meant to him. "Cat. After what just happened, you don't need an excuse to come see me."

She bit her lip, uncertain. "Right."

What was with the hesitation? Hadn't he made it clear how he felt about her? "Listen—"

"Okay," she said as if coming to a decision. "I believe you."

His brows shot up. "You believe me?"

"Yes." Her gaze swept over his body with such unabashed

admiration he almost pulled her back inside again. "Even though it's hard to believe."

"What's hard to believe? You're not making sense."

"I'd better dash," she said as she hurried to her car then she called over her shoulder, "Or I won't live to see you again."

Bryant watched her jump in her car and speed away. He didn't want to think about the future, but one thing he knew for certain: with Cat his life would never be boring.

33

Still alive?

Cat looked at the text from Bryant and managed a smile, although her ears were still ringing from her parents' shouts and laments. They bemoaned Ava's broken engagement and Maya's terrible influence on her sisters (although her eldest sister was now out of the house she was still blamed for most unfortunate events). They'd almost been forced to heat up leftovers! Didn't she care about their welfare?

Cat listened, nodded, profusely apologized and tried her best to appear remorseful.

Even though she didn't feel the tiniest grain of regret. Her body buzzing with joy, her mind taking flights away from the living room couch's stiff cushions to Bryant's soft bed linens, and the sensation of his hot skin against hers.

Eventually her parents grew tired of lecturing her and banished her to the kitchen where she made them a quick meal.

It was late when she finally escaped to her bedroom and saw Bryant's message. She sat on her bed and replied.

Barely. I made a lot of promises I won't be able to keep, but they're happy for now.

So I'll get to see you again.

She quickly typed *Yes, soon* then the image of a sexy black bra entered her thoughts and she deleted the words. She didn't want to be overeager. *I'll be busy for awhile.*

How long is awhile?

I'll let you know.

You are evil.

It gave her a little thrill that he wasn't shy expressing how much he wanted to see her again. Perhaps if she let him explain about the bra... She chewed her lips and typed:

Two weeks.

<sticker of a baby crying>

Cat laughed out loud at the image, then covered her mouth hoping no one had overheard her. Her parents wouldn't be pleased if she wasn't being repentant. When she didn't hear any footsteps coming to her door she typed *I've got a lot to make up for. I'll try to see what I can do.*

My father's visiting this week.

Oh, his father would be a perfect excuse if her parents wanted to know what she was up to. But it also sounded too perfect and convenient. *Is he really visiting?*

Does it matter?

It didn't matter.

Not at all. She'd lied to her parents before, but it felt even more important now. They didn't know about her life as Wicked Willa or her friendship with Vanessa or that she sometimes made up fake appointments so that she wouldn't have to be home, following the items on The List.

Even though she was careful, she always feared discovery. Feared the moment when one of her deceptions would be revealed.

But she never imagined she'd have a secret like this.

She loved every moment with him, but each time she left her heart grew heavier and heavier. She could lie to her parents but she couldn't lie to him.

So one afternoon, after a particularly amazing session with him, she slowly dressed and gathered her courage to end things.

"This has been better than I could have ever dreamed," she said tucking in her shirt.

Bryant sat up and narrowed his eyes. "Why does this sound like you're breaking up with me."

She sniffed at his wording. What was there to breakup? They hadn't made a commitment.

"I'm sorry." She sat on the edge of the bed and faced him. "I can't do this anymore. I don't want to share you. I want you all to myself."

"You have me."

"I know. When you're here, you're fully with me. But when I'm not here..." She shook her head. "I can't be one of your women."

Bryant shook his head. "I don't understand."

Cat reached under the mattress and pulled out the bra where she'd hid it. She held it out to him. "I found this."

Bryant fell upon it like it was a treasure. "Thank god. I've been looking all over for it."

"She must mean a lot to you."

"You have no idea," he said with feeling, running his finger across the hem. "Glad. It's not damaged."

His obvious relief and joy depressed her. So this really was just something casual between them? "Who is she?"

He turned the bra inside out. "Who is who?"

"The woman you're seeing."

"I'm not seeing anyone."

"You mean not anymore."

He looked up at her. "I'm sorry?"

Why did he have to make this difficult? "You obviously were seeing someone before me and now you're not. I was just curious who she was. And that's the problem because it's none of my business, right?"

"It's my mother's." Bryant held up his hand at Cat's look of shock. "No, no! Whatever you're thinking right now is so wrong—in too many ways to imagine." He shivered in horror. "I mean, this belongs to her but it's a project we've been working on." He took a deep breath. "Let me explain. My mum's a cardio-thoracic surgeon..." He then went on to tell Cat about his father's second wife and her misdiagnosed heart attack and that heart disease is still the number one killer of women. "I thought if there was a way to monitor a woman's heart it might save lives and a bra is one item of clothing most women wear." He then told her about how the tech-augmented bra could collect vital data, which the wearer could choose to share with their doctor.

"That sounds amazing."

"We've a ways to go, but I'm hopeful. My mum and I are not close, but it's been nice to work on something together and...wait. When did you find this?"

"The first time we were together."

"That's why," Bryant said with a look of relief. "I

thought..." He swore. "Cat, I don't want to be with anyone else but you."

She bit her lip. "You'll tell me when you change your mind?"

He drew her close and kissed her then whispered against her lips, "That won't happen any time soon."

But then a look entered his gaze. A familiar look, the same one she'd seen when she'd sat in his studio chair. Brief, but she saw it. It chilled the moment and they both knew it.

It was the look of fear.

Cat stood. "Perhaps I was right the first time. This won't work. I don't want you to be someone you're not ready to be."

Bryant reached for her. "Cat, it's not that."

She took a step back. "You don't have to torture yourself. If it's so hard to be with me—"

He shook his head, frustrated. "It's not you. I like being with you. Haven't I proven that?"

"Yes, but you still wished you didn't, right?"

He released a long sigh unable to deny it. "I'm not used to this, being this real, with anyone and a part of me hates it." He scrambled out of bed when she turned to the door. "No, don't go." He pulled her into his arms. "I want this. I really do."

"You're shaking."

"I know."

"If I really scare you this much..."

"It's not you."

"Yes it is," she said sadly.

"I admit you still scare me a bit." He paused. "No, that's wrong. It's not you. It's more my feelings about you than anything else. I hate being scared and I hate this feeling and I hate how weak I feel right now, but I hate the thought of losing you more. Of letting you go when you mean so much to me so…be patient. Okay?"

"You're not the only one who's scared, you know."

He sniffed. "But you like being scared."

"Not like this. This is new to me. No one's ever…" She turned in the circle of his arms and hugged him. "DH stands for Death-Hunter."

"What?"

"That's the nickname I gave you when I pictured you as a wrestler."

"Why Death-Hunter?"

"It's too complicated to explain, but it suited you. I even gave you a back story and choreographed your fights. You were amazing and of course won all the time."

"You are weird," he said with affection.

"I know, and I'm also an outsider who notices things. I know why you protect yourself and keep people at a distance. I hope that one day…maybe you'll learn to trust me. I'm not as scary as you think. I've never understood why you disliked me so much when I'd always wanted to know you better."

"Cat—"

"I'll never hurt you." She drew back. "When you're ready—"

He held her close, his breath warm on her neck. "I'm ready. I want this. I want you. I want us. Tell me what do you want me to do?"

"How about a date?"

34

He kept waiting for the shoe to drop.

Bryant held his breath as if awaiting a terrible, terrifying fate. He felt unsure of himself, unnatural in his own skin, horrified by how much hold of himself he'd given to another person. He awaited pain, suffering. Isn't that what love brought, wasn't that the risk that came with it? An almost monstrous vulnerability where the merest slight from a partner could feel like a knife wound?

Bryant glanced at the time then surged up from his chair and swore. He was supposed to meet with Cat almost forty minutes ago!

It'd been a week since they'd decided to start dating and he planned to take her to a café known for their desserts. Because of her schedule, dinner was impossible, they had to stick to the afternoons, and he couldn't take her too far in case she was needed at home or at one of the shops.

Today was to represent a major milestone and he'd already mucked it up. He vaguely remembered inviting her in, noticing that she had on a new fragrance that reminded him of pomegranates, and telling her to give him a few minutes to finish what he'd been working on. He never imagined he'd completely lose track of time.

He rushed into the living room and heard the screams of one of the characters (likely getting tortured or savaged since Cat liked to watch gruesome shows like that) and he felt as if it was his soul screaming at the realization of how much trouble he was in.

He must have made a sound because Cat quickly turned and said, "Close your eyes," before she grabbed the remote and stopped the movie. "I thought you were going to be another ten minutes."

He hadn't closed his eyes, but was glad she'd at least paused the movie so he didn't have to hear the screaming, although on the screen was the sight of a man with an axe through his arm.

He shoved his hands in his pockets and looked away, preparing for her wrath. "Why didn't you come get me?"

"You seemed to be on a role."

She didn't sound like she was criticizing him. He glanced at her. "You still should have told me."

She turned back to the screen. "Maybe."

Maybe? What did that mean? He looked at the shape of her head down to her slender neck, ready to feel resentful that this person who was barely half his size could have such a hold over him. She had every right to be angry at him. He'd experienced that before. Lovers who'd felt he'd neglected them. Soon she'd make him feel guilty and miserable and she had every right.

He gripped his hand into a fist determined to not let his resentment build. She hadn't done anything wrong; he wouldn't take his frustration out on her. He wanted this. He liked her. Although how he could fall for a woman who enjoyed seeing gruesome horror movies still baffled him. He'd apologize and—

"You came out for a snack, didn't you?" Cat said, leaping up from the couch.

"No," Bryant said confused by her matter-of-fact tone. "I came to take you out. For our date."

"It's a little too late for that."

He still couldn't believe he'd let the time pass him like that. This wasn't the side of him he'd wanted her to see yet. "I'm sorry. I—"

"You must be hungry. I've got just what you need. Stay there."

She disappeared into the kitchen then returned with a thermos and a glass container.

He stared at them. "What is this?"

"Tea and fresh ginger snaps."

He lifted his gaze to her face. "You're not angry?"

"I was," she said gently patting his cheek, "for about five minutes then I remembered you're weird too and only pretend not to be."

He didn't get to reply because his mobile rang and he had to deal with an issue with the web host for their account then a manufacturer alerted him to shipping delays for another product. He had a call with Keeden then an artist they'd hired who'd had to delay delivery because of a family emergency. By the time the day ended he hadn't had a chance to eat.

When he emerged from his study the sun had set. Cat had left a note that she'd gone home and would see him another time.

She'd not only made him a snack but had also scribbled

down an idea for a lunch he could make with leftovers she seen in the fridge.

It was the first time his house felt empty. He missed her.

They scheduled another time to be together, but it proved to be just as busy as the last. He apologized but she didn't seem bothered as she made herself comfortable on the couch.

It was then, watching that simple ordinary moment, that all his fears faded.

This was it.

This boringly simple moment, like many others he'd had in the past, was made sweeter because she was there. It wasn't surrender. She hadn't stolen anything from him. She'd given him something instead. A soft place of comfort in this changing world. A place of trust, sanctuary.

He thought of the snacks, the notes, the way she didn't bother him when he had to deal with business matters or was working on a project, how she understood him, how much he liked listening to her talk about her day at the shop or dealing with her parents.

They could still irritate each other, he knew they both were imperfect, but this choice, letting her past his walls, felt like the right choice. He wanted this person by his side.

There was nothing to fear about her or how he felt about her. There was no weakness in admitting that he didn't want to be alone.

He sat down beside her.

"All done?"

He sighed. "For now. Sorry, that our two dates have been ruined."

"I like this," she said. "Being in your house is so comforting. I never get to watch my movies on a big screen like this because even when I have a free moment, my parents hog the two that we have. Plus your fridge is always stocked."

"So you're using me for my house?"

"Of course. What else would there be? I mean it's not like you're a good looking, successful man with an amazing appreciation for my cooking or anything."

He rested a hand on her thigh. "You forgot a great lover."

"It's been awhile, I've forgotten."

He leaned forward. "Let me remind you," he said just as his cell phone rang.

He swore, she laughed.

He glared at her. "It's not funny."

"It's a busy time for you."

He looked at the phone to see if he could ignore it. He couldn't.

"I'm not going anywhere."

His brows shot up with hope. "You'll stay the night?"

"No, it means we can try this again. I'm in it for the long haul."

His phone fell silent as he let her words sink in. She wasn't going anywhere meant he didn't have to fear losing her.

He took a deep breath.

"I'm still going to try and cut this short," he said.

"You can try but you won't succeed."

Unfortunately, she was right. He read the note she'd left him and regretted that he hadn't planned things better, wished she didn't have to dash home every time they managed to find time together. He wanted things to be different.

The next time, he stayed out of his office, cleared his schedule determined that nothing would get in the way.

He planned a picnic at the local park.

It started to rain the moment he parked the car.

"It wasn't predicted," Bryant said, sending a resentful gaze up at the sky.

"There was a thirty percent chance," Cat said, looking at the weather app.

"Exactly."

"Which doesn't mean zero. You're such an optimist."

He leaned his head back. "This isn't working. It's been nearly a month and we've barely had real time together."

"I wouldn't say that."

"You said you wanted a date."

"This is a date. Let's eat what you packed and watch the rain fall. That sounds perfect to me. I enjoy just being with you. It doesn't have to be special."

He stared at her for a long moment, felt himself falling again. This was why. This moment, this time, this understanding. This was why he'd fallen for her and probably would keep falling. She made things feel okay. She calmed him. His ugly little angel.

"Okay, but the next time I see you. It's going to be better than this."

However, the next time she saw him was infinitely worse.

35

———

BECAUSE BRYANT HAD BECOME a master at disappearing, he rarely bumped into Cat at Keeden's house. The house was large enough and he always knew where to hide, what corridors to avoid, how not to get seen.

But Keeden forgot to warn him that Cat and Ava were coming by to visit Maya and that they'd planned to have lunch.

Bryant only found out when he left Keeden's studio and took a leisurely detour to the kitchen to make a quick snack before he left and nearly ran into Cat as she dashed out carrying a tray of sliced fruit.

She gasped.

He froze.

They stared at each other.

Neither knew what to do. Did they say anything? Pretend nothing had changed between them?

They didn't get a chance to speak when Keeden came up behind Bryant. "Uh oh. Back away slowly you two."

"Bryant," Maya called from the living room. "We're going

to have lunch. You've been such a help to me and we have more than enough food. Please join us."

He opened his mouth but no words came out.

Keeden rested a hand on his friend's shoulder and said in a quiet voice, "Just endure it for me."

He cast a glance at Cat then beamed at Maya. "Sure, why not?"

Fortunately, the large patio table gave them enough distance and Bryant made sure to sit diagonal to Cat. He easily slipped into character and charmed everyone with his radiant smile and light hearted manner. So much so that no one commented on Cat, who had barely touched her food and kept picking up her glass and putting it down without taking a sip. Although the summer heat had given way to a muted autumn breeze, Cat felt so hot she feared she'd sweat through her shirt.

"It's nice to see you relaxed, Bryant," Maya said, after he'd made them all laugh with a story about a temperamental client. "The Old Woman says you always seem to be working."

Bryant's practiced smile almost slipped. Lena. Of course. He'd offered to see her at one of her sports events but then had to cancel. "Yes, well I've been working on a couple of projects."

"What do you do in your spare time?" Maya asked.

"Watch videos of panda's playing in the snow," Keeden said.

"No, really?"

Bryant's smile slowly dimmed, he sent his friend a sharp glance. "It's nothing."

Keeden grinned. "Hours."

"That's not true."

Maya and Ava giggled.

"I didn't know pandas liked to play in the snow," Maya said.

"Doesn't it get boring?" Ava asked.

"I think it sounds nice," Cat said.

They all turned to her surprised.

"What?" she said unfazed by their reaction. "People bird watch or look at cat videos. What's the difference?"

"Pandas in the snow is kind of specific," Maya said.

"Yes, but it sounds soothing," Cat said. Her gaze briefly met his. "Is it?"

Bryant nodded. "I find it comforting."

"You would." She grinned at him. A grin he used to find haughty and superior but now appeared understanding instead.

"Personally, I'd use it as a sleep aid," Keeden said.

"Oh, speaking of sleep," Cat said. "Did you know chickpeas are good for that and I roasted some but I forgot them in the kitchen."

"I'll get them," Bryant said, standing.

Cat stared at him surprised. "But—"

"I don't mind." He came around the table. "Chat with your sisters," he said before giving her shoulder a tender squeeze before he left.

"I'll help," Keeden said, following.

Cat looked at her sisters.

They stared back opened mouthed.

She bit into an apple slice trying her best to ignore them.

"What. Was. *That*?" Maya asked.

"He didn't know what he was doing," Cat mumbled.

"He touched you on purpose."

"It's not a big deal."

"What's going on?"

"Nothing."

"He's changed."

"It's because I taught him a recipe and he's thankful. That's all."

Her sister's looked doubtful. "A recipe?" Maya said.

"Yes. I've been helping him out, but don't say anything 'cause you'll embarrass him."

Her sister's mouths fell open again.

Cat held out her hands. "What?"

"You don't want to embarrass him?" Ava said.

"When tormenting—," Maya said.

"—harassing—," Ava added.

"—and teasing him—"

"Have been one of your favorite pastimes?"

"It's just this one time," Cat said.

Maya clapped her hands together as a thought struck her. "I know. You lost a bet, didn't you?"

Ava grinned. "That's right. It has to be why you're acting this way."

Cat rubbed the back of her neck. "Yeah, that's right. He didn't want me to ruin this lunch for you."

"I knew it," Maya said.

"But then what did he just whisper in your ear?"

While Cat racked her thoughts in search of a reply, in the kitchen, Keeden stared at his friend amazed.

"Is something wrong?" Keeden asked him. "Is Uncle okay?"

Bryant put the roasted chickpeas into a serving bowl, resisting the urge to take a few. "Yes, why?"

"You don't think this afternoon is strange?"

He frowned. "What's strange about it? Maya invited me over for lunch."

"With her sisters."

"Right."

"Her *sisters*," Keeden said, emphasizing the last word in case Bryant hadn't notice.

"I know."

"You've never said yes before. Ever. You avoid them, mainly Cat, as if she's contagious."

Bryant paused as if finally realizing what his friend was saying. "Hmm."

"But now you're treating her like..."

"Like what?" Bryant pressed when Keeden fell silent.

He sighed. "I know it's tricky and I know what you're trying to do. Especially since the incident with her parents. But you don't have to overcompensate. I know this is hard for you."

"Hard?"

"She's hardly eaten anything. That's not like her. And she looks at you as if she's afraid of something. Tell it to me straight. Did you threaten her?"

"What?"

"I know how you can be. What you're capable of. And I know you'll stand up for me and wouldn't want anything to jeopardize my relationship with Maya. But I also know Cat and she's never been this quiet before. Tell me what's going on."

"I didn't threaten her."

"But you did something. She's not acting like herself and neither are you. Did you find out why she's been shopping with your dad?"

"No."

"Well, either ask her or let it go. You keep staring at her. I want you to cut it out."

Bryant hesitated, unsure of how much he should share.

"I'm trying to be a different person. Your feelings for Maya changed and I thought—"

"The bad blood between Maya and me came down to a misunderstanding, but you..." Keeden shook his head. "You and Cat aren't even oil and water. You're gasoline and lighter fluid. You've avoided and hated this woman for years and pretending that you don't is making everyone nervous. Cut the BS, okay?"

Bryant lifted the serving bowl. "Fine."

Fortunately for Cat, Bryant and Keeden returned before she had to come up with a reply to her sister's question. Bryant flashed one of his beautiful smiles as he set the food on the table.

He sat down and looked at the women sensing a change. "What?"

Maya and Ava shared a look.

"What was the bet?" Maya finally said.

Bryant frowned. "Bet?"

"That Cat lost."

"We know that's the only way you'd get her to act like this."

Bryant looked at Cat. *Should we tell them?*

Cat looked at Bryant and nodded before she said, "Actually, we're dating."

36

Ava, Maya and Keeden burst into laughter.

Their laughter hurt. It shouldn't have. Cat knew that she and Bryant made an odd pair. But it hurt all the same. That something so precious and dear to her could be the source of amusement, even mockery, from people who loved her, cracked her heart a bit.

So she forced a chuckle and said, "Ridiculous, right?"

Ava nodded. "You always come up with the strangest things to say."

"Next you'll try to convince us you're in love with each other," Maya said.

They laughed harder.

Bryant didn't laugh. He didn't smile either. He rested an arm on the back of the chair beside him, which made him appear even larger and broader than he was.

Keeden was the first to notice the change on his friend's face then Maya and Ava and their laughter quickly subsided into a silent unease. When Bryant stopped smiling people didn't know what to do. He drummed his fingers and cut the tension in the air with a smile, as sharp as a machete. "I know it sounds funny, but she's not joking."

They all looked at Cat and Maya said, "You're not joking?"

Cat shook her head. "No."

"But that's impossible," Ava said. "You have nothing in common."

"After my father's fall," Bryant said aware Keeden wasn't to find out the truth about Mrs. Kayode's cooking and Cat's involvement, "Cat helped me with some things and we discovered we have more in common than we first thought."

The trio stared at Bryant and Cat unable to know what to say.

"I know it's a lot to take in," Cat said.

Ava looked distressed. "But Mom will never let you—"

Maya rested a hand on Ava's stopping her words. "We're happy for you."

"The parents don't know yet," Cat said.

"Of course. They won't hear anything from us." Maya gently squeezed Ava's hand and she quickly nodded in agreement although her eyes looked sad.

Bryant rested his arms on the table. "But one day we'll have to tell them—"

"No!" all three sisters said in unison.

"It's too soon," Maya said, trying her best to soften their response.

Ava shook her head. "No, it's not that. It's because Mom —" She stopped when Maya shot her a look. "Right...it's too soon."

Before Bryant could reply, Ava's phone alerted her to a text. "Oh, it's Dai. I have to go."

"I'll walk you out," Cat said.

Once they were outside, she said. "You don't have to worry about me, Ava. I know what I'm doing."

Ava stopped and turned to her. Her sweet face looked sad. "Cat, I'm so sorry. We didn't mean to laugh."

"It's okay. I know it's hard to believe, I haven't always liked him this much," Cat said with a laugh to cover up her embarrassment. She knew they made an odd pair. "Anyway, it can't last, but right now I'm happy."

Ava hugged her. "You deserve it."

Cat watched her go then returned inside, wondering how best to reassure Maya. But only Keeden remained on the patio. "Maya and Bryant went to the studio to talk over a project they're working on," he informed her.

"Oh." She began to gather some of the dishes.

"Leave it," he said standing. "I hire people to do that for me."

"But—"

Keeden walked inside and said over his shoulder, "Mathilde is more than efficient and she knew I was having guests. Don't insult her or me."

Cat set the dishes down and followed him. It was best to do so because it was easy to get lost in the labyrinth of corridors and stairs in the grand house.

Keeden wasn't a tall man and his slender build and two long braids could put someone under the false impression he was weak, until you met his gaze and realized how commanding, powerful and clever he truly was.

In the pro wrestling world she'd cast him as a heel, he'd make a remarkable villain, and she knew he'd relish the role. Unlike Bryant, Keeden didn't care what people thought of him. One always got a sense he'd rather be somewhere else. That he didn't enjoy people, but rather tolerated them.

He led her to the casual living room and sat before he gazed out the window. He never tried to fill silences, but settled comfortably into them. While Bryant could make a room feel smaller and cozier, Keeden had the opposite effect. He could make a room feel larger and intimidating.

Cat rubbed her hands on her thighs unsure what to do. Did he want to stay silent? Did he want her to tell him more about her relationship with Bryant? Did he...

"So, you're the reason," Keeden said with a sly grin as if he'd uncovered the solution to a puzzling mystery.

"The reason?"

Keeden clicked his tongue in pity. "That's why he kept staring. Damn, that's why he was going on about being a different person. He was trying to tell me and I didn't listen. I can't believe I got it so wrong."

"I don't understand."

Keeden rubbed his chin. "I never thought he'd fall this hard."

"Fall for me?" Cat said shocked. "No way. It's not like that at all." She waved her hands. "You've got it all wrong."

Keeden turned to her, pinning her with a penetrating stare. "Do I?"

"Y-yes," she said, suddenly uncertain. She sat up gathering courage. She wouldn't let him make her question herself. She knew what she was doing and what to expect from Bryant. "We have a great time, but sometimes I'm not sure he even likes me."

Keeden leaned back with a knowing, secretive expression. "He likes you all right. Very much."

"You don't know that."

"Yes, I do."

"A few moments ago you didn't even think we were a couple."

He sighed with regret and swore. "That's because the bastard's good. I was completely fooled." He shook his head with a note of admiration. "Really good."

"Exactly," Cat said seizing on his words. "He's a great pretender. You can't always know how he feels."

Keeden leaned forward, clasping his hands together. "It's not like you to lie to yourself."

"I'm not lying."

"Then why are you trying to talk yourself out of a serious relationship? We both know it's serious. If it was casual, you'd know it. Bryant doesn't play those games." Keeden lifted his forefinger. "One time. He's only been this serious about a woman *one time* and it was for all the wrong reasons. But you're different."

She wanted to believe him, but Cat still had her doubts. And she felt uncomfortable. She wasn't used to talking about her feelings like this so she decided to make light of it. "Flattery will get you anything."

"I'm not flattering you, I'm telling you the truth."

"*I* can't handle the truth," she said reworking a famous movie line.

"Does he scare you?"

She didn't want to talk about it and all he'd told her about Bryant made her uncomfortable. It couldn't be serious with Bryant because it couldn't last. And there was no way he could want... She began to stand. "It's late—"

"It's not that late."

"But my parents—"

"You're at my house. I can have you spend the night if I wanted to and they wouldn't bat an eyelash."

He was right. Unlike Bryant, Keeden knew his power in their community and how to use it. He was an Adesina after all.

She sank back into her seat and tried to change the subject. "I wonder how long Maya and Bryant will be?"

"I asked you a question."

Damn. Why wouldn't he let it drop? "What was the question again?"

"How soon do you plan to break his heart?"

"That wasn't the question."

He grinned. "It is now."

"I'd never do that."

"Yes, you will."

"I wouldn't. Why would you say that?"

"Because you don't really care about him."

"Of course I care. I might not be lovey-dovey and such but I do."

"Then why do you question how he feels about you?"

"I told you," she said losing patience, "because he can be hard to read. I promise you, our relationship is not as serious as you think."

Keeden folded his arms. "Why would you think that?"

"Because he's never smiled at me. Really smiled."

Keeden stared at her for a long moment then threw his head back and laughed.

Cat surged to her feet. "You think that's funny?"

"No, no," he said quickly. "I'm not laughing at you. I swear. Sit down. Sit *down*." He bit his lip, trying to tame his amusement, as Cat cautiously took a seat. "I'm sorry. It's...you're seeing the real him. That's Bryant. The real Bryant doesn't smile.

"The first time I met him I felt the same way you do. I was

shocked he wanted to be friends. He'd always looked so pissed and annoyed. Everything else about him, that charm, that grin? It's something he's had to work on. You're one of the few people he's being truly honest with. Truly himself. He's a serious guy who worries a lot—"

"And hates being scared."

Keeden rubbed his chin and looked as if he was going to say something but decided against it. He nodded. "Right. His smiles are his shield, he uses them to keep people at a distance. He wasn't sure anyone would like him otherwise. So he's being himself with you. I hope you can handle that."

"I'm going to make it a challenge. I'm going to get him to smile."

"Don't be fooled. When he's with you, he smiles in all the ways that matter." Keeden sent her a long considering look. "One day, ask him about his angel."

37

____

Bryant's hand felt warm and solid in hers as he walked her to her car.

"You don't have to go," Bryant said when they stopped in front of her car. "Keeden said he'd cover for us." He bent down and placed a kiss on her neck, his voice warm against her skin when he said, "and he has enough rooms."

"Tempting," Cat said backing away, "but I really have a lot to do. Maybe another time."

A flash of something—dark, guarded—entered his gaze.

Does he scare you?

Keeden's question rose in her thoughts. It wasn't Bryant who filled her with terror (a delicious, spine-tingling terror); it was her feelings for him that scared her. They were so deep, so all-encompassing and the thought of one day having to let him go...

"Okay," he said and then he began to smile and that was the last thing she wanted to see. Now she knew he only did it to protect himself. He was protecting himself from her.

Protecting himself from getting hurt. She realized they were both scared.

But she didn't mind a little fear.

She drew him close and kissed the false smile away, indulging in the succulent taste of his lips and the sweet danger of completely falling in love with him, before she said, "I really wish I could stay, but..." But what? Damn... if only she was better with words, better at making him feel at ease, but she could only tell him the truth. She leaned closer and lowered her voice, "I'm still in trouble. I was thinking about you the other day and I ended up burning my mother's sheets."

Bryant frowned. "Why are you ironing her sheets?"

"Thank God I caught an error in the accounting that made up for it, barely. But then I forgot to point out a stain to the dry cleaners on *two* of Dad's shirts and ended up having to hand-wash them. Then the cookies I made for her book club were not my best. And I've been practicing with Vanessa for our upcoming performance."

His frown deepened. "Cat, you can't keep this up."

"I can and I will." She threw her arms around his neck and grinned up at him. "Because if I keep them happy then I get to see you."

"Cat—"

"It's fine." She almost laughed at the worry she saw in his gaze. Yes, this was the Bryant she knew. "So I have to be careful a little while longer. I'll use the 'Keeden card' on a real special occasion. Like Guy Fawkes Day."

"Hmm."

"That was a joke."

"It wasn't funny."

She made a face.

He trailed a finger along her jaw. "Thanks for not laughing."

"About what?"

"The pandas."

She shrugged. "I think it's sweet." She opened her car door. "Can I buy you a stuffed one?"

"No."

She turned to him surprised. "Why not?" When he didn't readily reply she read his face and started to grin. "Because you already have one."

He shook his head. "That's not it."

"I'm going to find a cute little—"

"I don't want one."

"Why not?"

His gaze shifted away then he said in a low voice, "Because stuffed animals scare me."

She rested against the doorframe and started to laugh.

"I'm not kidding."

"Cute little—"

"They're not cute. They have these eyes, these dark beady eyes that are..." He shivered unable to continue. "I don't like them or action figures or dolls. Anything with a face."

She nodded. "I can see how dolls can be terrifying. Especially the way they're used in movies. But a stuffed toy..."

"We're not having this discussion."

She sat in the driver's seat. "How bad is it? Do you break out in a sweat or something?"

"I was attacked once. I was at a show and it jumped on me."

"You mean fell."

"No jumped, the guy making it talk was with it."

"A puppet is different than a stuffed toy."

"I don't care. I was traumatized for life."

She took his hand. "You poor little thing."

"I still have nightmares," he said his hand slowly creeping up her arm, sending shivers, his voice deepened to a velvet tone. "But only when I'm alone."

Cat pulled her hand away, seeing through his ploy. "I'm not staying."

Bryant stepped away and let his voice return to normal. "Worth a shot."

"I'll try to see you next week."

"Try very hard."

However, no matter how hard Cat tried she didn't get to see him that week. And barely the week following. Because of a flurry of activities that crowded both their schedules, they were forced to find, brief stolen moments to be together. Until sparkling eye shadow and purple lipstick finally gave them a chance to be together.

38

———

"Hold still."

"I'm trying."

Bryant sat back and set the eyeliner down with satisfaction. They sat at his dining room table, where the array of makeup he'd bought lay spread out on the table. He lifted his mobile and took a picture. "You're ready."

Cat stared at the image of herself amazed. "I almost look beautiful."

"You don't need to be beautiful when you're interesting."

"I'd kiss you, but I'd ruin this amazing design." She stood. She wore silver trousers and a blood red blouse with flowing sleeves. "I'd better get going."

Bryant nodded, looking a little sad.

"What is it?"

"Too bad your man is too much of a coward to see you perform."

Cat struck a fierce pose, resting a hand on her hip. "Any man who can handle this is not a coward."

Bryant stood. "Still can't believe you used the Keeden card for this event instead of a night with me."

"Mom was determined to host an impromptu event I knew I wouldn't have time to prepare for, I was desperate. Usually when I tell her I have a class or I'm volunteering somewhere, she believes me. But this time, it's almost like—"

"Like what?"

She knows I'm trying to break free of her. To have my own life. "Nothing. Besides I was able to spend nearly four hours with you. That's something."

"Half the time you were getting ready for the show."

She winked, playfully drawing a circle on his chest. "But the other half..." She let her words fall away so that he could remember how they'd spent those hours together: The sex, the food, the sex.

"Didn't feel long enough," he grumbled.

She blew him a kiss. "I will make it up to you, I promise."

"I'll hold you to it. Text me when the show's over."

"I will." She turned.

"Wait, let me take a few more pictures."

"If you make me late—"

"You won't be late." Bryant took a few pictures of her and then a couple of them together. He looked down at the final image satisfied. Cat peered over his shoulder in her Wicked Willa persona and he looked at the camera as if it was the most normal thing in the world. To others the picture would look like a shocking contrast, but to him, it looked, "Perfect."

Later that evening, Bryant received an unsatisfying, *Great night,* text from Cat and little else. He waited for more, but suspected she was too busy to get back to him, especially when the texts he sent didn't receive a reply.

He had to resist pulling Gareth out of the car when the young man arrived at Bryant's house with his dad.

"I need to talk to you," Bryant said once he'd welcomed his father and watched him enter the house. "It's nothing bad," he added when Gareth looked nervous. Which was a relief for both of them. Bryant's dad had stayed out of trouble and the shopping trips with Cat had stopped.

"Can we talk out here?" Gareth said.

"Why?"

He cast a glance at the house as if it were a gothic castle lit by moonlight. "'Cause your house is so—"

"I once spilled ketchup on the carpet and guess what? The house didn't fall down. Amazing engineering that."

Gareth scowled. "That's not what I mean."

"How was Cat's show?"

"Cat?"

"Wicked Willa."

His eyes grew wide with excitement and he started bouncing on his toes. "Oh man..."

Bryant turned and walked inside.

Gareth eagerly followed unaware he was being led to the living room he feared as he described the events of the evening.

He sat down on the couch and ate one of the crackers and cheese Bryant had on the coffee table, all the while sharing about the music and the costumes. "Totally amazing. I mean there was this scene where a guy gets knifed in the—"

Bryant shook his head. "Don't want to know. Don't need details. Just a general review."

"They hit it. It got a little wild at one point, but it was fine."

"Wild how?"

"This guy leaped on the stage, you know, and went for Hazzy but Wicked Willa wasn't having it and, you gotta understand she stayed cool and kept playing but she stuck her leg out and tripped him and he went down like Bam!" Gareth made the motion as if he were squashing a bug between his hands. "Fortunately, the guy was too drunk to get back up again and was hauled off the stage."

"And she's all right?"

"All right? You wouldn't have thought anything happened. She's got veins of ice. Too bad you couldn't be there."

"Yeah." He felt the same. He let Gareth rattle on a little while longer then shifted the discussion to his dad. Thankfully, Gareth had nothing new to report, except that his father had bought two new shirts.

"Both white," Gareth said with a shake of his head. "You'd think he didn't know they made them in other colors."

Bryant nodded. "It's an obsession."

They parted ways then Bryant checked on his father and had a brief chat with him before he went to his studio to work.

But he couldn't focus. He picked up his phone and sent Cat a text.

Heard about the drunk guy.

Highlight of my night.

You sure you're all right?

Yes. Imagined he was one of those Georgia guys who'd beat you up. Seeing him go down was a thrill.

Sorry I didn't text back sooner.

It's okay.

Next week is swamped. But I'll see what I can do after that.

His heart sank. Not because he was disappointed (he was) or that he missed her (that too) but because Cat was finding it harder and harder to find a free moment. It was as if her parents were tightening their grip on her. There were times he'd find her asleep on the couch when she came over to visit. Other times he saw dark circles under her eyes from lack of sleep. He didn't like how they were pushing her.

He began to type, *Maybe we should tell them about us,* then deleted the message knowing she wouldn't agree. He didn't like feeling helpless, but knew she couldn't keep up this pace. He didn't want their relationship to be a burden to her.

That's fine. My week's busy too, he replied before he set down the phone and leaned back in his chair. He didn't like having to lie.

He couldn't keep pretending like this. He had to assess what was really going on.

That meant meeting the opposition.

39

———

THE RUSE WAS simple but brilliant.

Bryant showed up at the Kayode house, meeting a surprised and beautifully dressed Mrs. Kayode at the door, explaining to her he was there for Mrs. Adesina. With his charming smile and the mention of an old family name Mrs. Kayode had no choice but to welcome him inside, although she was clearly not prepared for unexpected guests.

Fortunately, his easy manner removed her anxiety and he explained he was in the neighborhood and had offered to pick up some cloth for Mrs. Adesina as a favor. He'd heard about Mrs. Adesina and Mrs. Kayode's ongoing exchanges through Cat and decided to insert himself as the middleman instead of having Cat do her usual role of shuttling items between the families.

Mrs. Kayode began to gesture towards the living room for him to sit while she got the cloth, but savory smells, floating down the hallway, lured him away. Bryant disarmed her by sharing his love of her culinary skills, his admiration and smile making her blush like a young girl, while he made his way to the kitchen.

What he saw wiped the smile from his face. Platters full of food crowded the countertop, the level of work looked to be the effort of at least four people, all done by one person dashing to and fro.

His gaze fell on a cutting board with vegetables ready to be chopped and Cat looking more harried and worn than he'd ever seen her.

While Mrs. Kayode looked every bit the lady of the manor, Cat in contrast, wore dingy jeans and a faded sweater with frayed edges. She wiped sweat from her forehead then halted like a startled antelope when she saw him.

His anger arrived with such swift ferocity that when he cast an unguarded look at Mrs. Kayode it held the sting of venom so biting that the older woman winced as if he'd sunk his teeth into her flesh. He quickly regained control, banked down his feelings and hid behind a mask once more. "I apologize. I didn't realize you were busy."

"Yes, quite," Mrs. Kayode said, smoothing back her hair, although her beautiful face needed no such improvement. "But we're managing. We have more guests arriving than we'd expected, so Cat's helping me."

Bryant rolled up his sleeves. "Tell me what you need."

A look of horror crossed her face. "Oh, we're fine as we are—"

"Please," he said with a smile that held the sharp edge of a threat rather than a request.

Mrs. Kayode looked towards Cat silently asking what she should say. Cat sent a pointed glance at the cutting board. Mrs. Kayode returned her attention to Bryant and motioned to the vegetables. "You can chop those."

"Any particular way?"

"No," Cat said, smoothly rescuing her mother without shaming her. "Mom's not picky."

He nodded then washed his hands and reviewed the selection of knives.

While Bryant calmly looked at the cutlery, Cat stared at his broad back in a mild panic. What was he doing??? Why was he there?

Her mother's discreet cough pulled her back to the present and she returned her attention to the pinwheel appetizers.

She didn't know what he was thinking, but could tell he wasn't happy. Why had he decided to stop by without telling her? What good did he think it would do?

She briefly closed her eyes in dread when Bryant began muttering to himself saying things like 'ridiculous' and 'utter nonsense.' He then went on about responsible planning and time management, nothing too revealing (he could be talking about his business for all they knew) until she overheard him say, "Things will be different when we're married."

Cat cast a furtive look at her mother who continued to sort the glasses as if she hadn't heard and Bryant hadn't realized he'd said anything aloud.

Cat excused herself and left the kitchen, her legs like lead, her heart pounding. She stumbled outside and collapsed on one of the patio chairs. She didn't know what to think.

Marriage? Was Bryant really considering marriage?

Her mother had pointedly ignored his words, which had been loud enough for them both to overhear. But of course her mother ignored most things related to Cat. She'd dismiss them as unreal. She wouldn't imagine Bryant was talking about Cat. It had to be someone else. Who would want to marry her?

And it had been a throwaway comment. Bryant always

said odd things when he was talking to himself. She couldn't take what he'd said seriously.

A shadow descended over her. She turned and saw Bryant. Her heart filled with joy and she gripped her hands into fists so she wouldn't jump into his arms and fall into the safety of his solid embrace. She didn't know why he was there, but she was glad to see him.

"Are you okay?" he asked.

Did you mean what you said? Do you even know what you said?

Cat tugged on her sweater. "Kitchen was a little stuffy. I needed some air."

He handed her a glass of water. "You need more than air."

"What are you doing here?"

He pressed the glass in her hand and mumbled, "Trying to understand the enemy."

She blinked. "What?"

He shook his head. "Never mind." He closed her fingers around the glass. "Take it."

Cat drew the glass to her lips and whispered against the rim, "Death-Hunter."

He narrowed his eyes.

She giggled. "Don't do that. You look as if you're ready to put someone in an ambulance."

He rested his hands on his hips. "Which is not far from wrong." He nodded to the glass. "Drink."

She hesitated and glanced over her shoulder. "Does she know you're out here with me?"

"Relax, she doesn't suspect a thing. You could sit on my lap, with your arms wrapped around my neck and I doubt she'd bat an eyelash."

Cat laughed at the apt description, feeling her worries

subside. She drank the water then handed it back to him. "My hero."

He took the glass and frowned. "Cat, what she's making you do is impossible. You really can't—"

The worry and concern in his gaze wanted to make her drown him in questions about what he'd said, how he felt, what he meant, but she knew it was dangerous. It wasn't safe with her mother looming and able to pounce at any moment.

She stood, interrupting him. "I'm all right now." She took the glass from him and nudged him to the door. "You'd better go."

40

———

"Haven't seen Cat in a while," Bryant's father said, sitting back in his chair, smoothing down the front of the pristine white shirt Bryant had bought him for Christmas. He'd waited until New Year's Day to wear it.

I haven't seen her either, Bryant wanted to say, drumming his fingers on his dining room table. Autumn had turned to winter and he'd seen Cat only once—for an afternoon snack that had all the hallmarks of speed dating.

They exchanged a speckling of texts, some sweet video memos, but that was all they could manage. Their usual ploys, mentioning his father or Keeden, didn't have the same effect anymore persuading her parents to give her space. He hadn't even been able to give her the Christmas gift he'd bought for her.

Bryant watched his father take another sandwich cookie—Nutella slathered between two crisp shortbread cookies. Cat had suggested it, promising a hazelnut, chocolate treat, and he wished she'd been able to enjoy it with them.

He'd enjoyed the quiet New Year's dinner with his father,

but as he stared at the plate full of cookies he felt a sense of dread he'd never had before, a painful longing. Cat should be there and his father felt it too.

He could blame the holidays, it was always a busy time, but he sensed something more sinister keeping them apart. Something more calculated and cunning. If he didn't do something soon, he'd lose her.

"You should invite her over," his father said.

I've tried. He picked up one of the cookies. "I will." He stood. He didn't want to talk about Cat and didn't want to get annoyed with his father for bringing her up. "I know a movie we can watch."

It put them both to sleep. Only the sound of his mobile ringing managed to rouse him. He absently reached for it and answered. "Yes?"

Cat's voice came through. "I'm sorry to wake you."

Bryant sat up, instantly alert. "What's wrong?" He rushed into the hallway so that he wouldn't wake his father. "Are you okay?"

"Yes, I'm fine. I'm outside."

"Outside?"

"Outside your house."

He raced to the door and swung it open, the winter night rushed in chilling his skin.

But the sight of Cat made it burn.

"I know it's late," she said. "I had to sneak out, but I wanted to see y—"

Her lips were cold pressed against his, her cheeks were freezing and all he could think about was warming her up: Wrapping his body around her, filling her with his heat, keeping her close.

When he drew away from her lips, Cat smiled and said, "Hmm, you taste like chocolate and hazelnut."

She tasted like luscious forbidden fruit—ripe, ready, juicy. She wasn't supposed to be there and that made everything feel even more divine.

He wouldn't waste a minute.

They made it to his bedroom without waking his father. They made it to the bed, clothes left discarded in their wake, without saying another word.

In many ways Cat was still braver and bolder than he was. She still took more risks, but from the way she responded to him— the gentle moans, the writhing arousal—he'd made the risk worth it. Although Bryant knew they didn't have much time, he still didn't rush. He wanted to savor every touch, scent, flavor of her and she responded the same, indulging in the moment as if he were the finest dessert.

But still, too soon, she had to go.

Bryant trailed a finger down Cat's back as she sat on the side of the bed and fastened her bra. She smiled at him over her shoulder. "Happy New year."

He laughed. "It is now." He sat up. "How did you manage to get out of the house?"

"It's a secret." She pulled on her jeans. "But wouldn't be the first time I've run away." She chuckled. "And the first time led me to you."

"What do you mean?"

"I know that day was painful for you—"

"It's okay, tell me."

"We were visiting family in Georgia and there were lots of cousins and aunts and uncles and I felt invisible and I was miserable for a number of reasons I won't bore you with. Anyway, I thought I'd runaway. I packed my things and just started walking. I don't know how far I'd gone when I spotted your father get off the bus.

"He did the strangest thing. He smiled and waved at me. Nobody did that. I was such an odd looking kid most people either didn't see me or looked away. I was an embarrassment to my parents. Anyway, your dad probably shouldn't have done that because like a baby duck I followed him. I don't know why. Even when he met you at the school, I still followed. You didn't notice me and I didn't care. You both looked so happy I envied you and also saw what was possible. That happiness was real. It sometimes felt like everyone around me only pretended to be happy.

"Who knows where I would have ended up if we hadn't crossed paths. I'm glad I did because then..." She sighed and shook her head reluctant to rehash the painful moment.

"At the hospital I saw a cousin who was a nurse. He would have recognized me so I gave up the idea of running away. The amazing thing is after everything that happened, I returned home and nobody realized I'd been gone. But I didn't care because you and your dad made me feel useful. I was proud of myself."

"You were an amazing kid. My hero." Bryant drew her close and pressed his lips against hers then whispered, "Can I show you how grateful I am?"

Cat laughed and wiggled out of his grasp. "You already have."

"I can show you some more."

"Next time." She headed for the door.

Next time would be too far in the future. He didn't want to wait that long. Bryant jumped out of bed, coming to a decision. "Before you go, I have to show you your Christmas gift."

41

———

SHE DIDN'T SEE it at first.

When Bryant quietly led Cat into the kitchen, after putting a blanket over his still sleeping father, everything looked exactly as she'd always remembered it.

Then she saw it: A small apron hanging next to the pantry, beside his.

She walked over to it. "What's this?"

"It's yours." Bryant took the apron down and draped it over her head before tying the string behind her back. "You can cook here anytime you want."

It was tantamount to him giving her the keys to his house. A bold move. "Thank you."

"I don't make this offer lightly."

"I know," she said, gazing down at the apron in awe.

"So you can spot a proposal when you hear one?"

She spun around and stared at him. "You're not serious."

"I never joke about my kitchen."

She stared down at the apron. "But this is...I never imagined..." She stared up at him. "Are you sure? Do you know what you're doing? Do you know what this means? Are you asking me to marry you?"

He nodded. He looked serious. More serious than she'd ever seen him before.

Cat bit her lip then nodded. Yes, she'd marry him, no question, but what would she do about her parents? "I have to think about it." She untied the apron and hung it up. "Right now I have to go."

Bryant briefly looked disappointed then resigned. "Okay."

He followed her to the front door. "Take your time making up your mind, but don't keep me waiting too long."

"Oh, I've already made up my mind. I want to marry you."

"But you said you have to think about it."

"Yes," she said in a grave tone, "I have to think about how we'll make it happen. If it's even possible."

Bryant frowned. "I don't understand."

"I can't say 'yes' until I figure out how to convince my parents to let me marry you."

"I'm not a stranger. They already know me. Why don't you stay until the morning and then we'll face your parents together and—"

"No, we can't do that. She'd—" Cat stopped. She didn't want to reveal what her mother was capable of. Bryant had no idea the kind of person he'd be facing. It might scare him off. It was best she handle this one on her own. She'd been managing her mother for years; this would be a crucial test. "It's going to be difficult. No one ever expected I would...I mean even I didn't think I...and now..." She sighed. "Trust me on this, okay?"

"I trust you." He cupped her chin. "Just remember you can also trust me."

Sensing disaster had become a skill.

A skill Cat had become a master at avoiding, but this time she would be the cause, if she didn't handle things right.

Telling her sisters about marrying Bryant was out of the question, she couldn't have anyone even accidentally alert her parents to what she wanted to do. Plus she couldn't trust Gwen, her mother couldn't stand Maya and Ava's broken engagement and new relationship was still a sore spot.

Telling her parents about marrying Bryant had to be strategic. She couldn't do it the traditional formal way. It would have been easy to tell them over dinner, have both her parents together and get it over with in one blow.

But then the odds would be against her. Two against one and she'd be trapped.

She considered pleading. But she wasn't humble enough for that.

The third option seemed the best. A surprise attack.

The early morning rush seemed the best strategy, they always left for work together and functioned on autopilot.

Cat waited for her father to open the front door, and nodded dutifully as her mother left instructions for the day before Cat said, "Yes, I understand and I'm getting married."

Her father nodded and her mother said, "Good," before she closed the door.

Cat held her breath. Had she really gotten away with it? Would it be that simple? She was used to being ignored and they had so much on their minds...

The door flew open.

She met the beautiful cold glare of a predator.

"Repeat that," her mother said in a too soft tone.

"I'm getting married."

"That's what I thought you said."

"Who—?" her father began but her mother held up her hand stopping his words. "We'll discuss this when we get home."

She closed the door.

Disaster was on its way.

And it came with the scent of peaches. Her mother had returned from the spa smelling extra fragrant. Her father smelled like cinnamon coffee.

They both faced her in the living room where they'd told her to join them.

"I didn't think you were so eager to abandon us," her mother said.

Cat waited. She wanted to deny the accusation but knew it'd be fruitless. It was best to let her mother say her piece.

"You're young. Why would you want to marry so soon? Gwen and Ava waited. Although in Ava's case that might have been a mistake, but that's neither here nor there. What you're thinking is ridiculous. Is it jealousy?"

Cat sighed, still not time to speak.

"Of course it is," her mother continued. "What else could it be? One daughter shames me, another breaks off a perfectly excellent engagement and now you have decided to abandon us for some random man—"

"I'm not abandoning you."

Her mother scowled, her father said, "Don't interrupt your mother."

Cat nodded, feigning remorse. "I'm sorry."

"What are we supposed to do?" her mother said. "Haven't we treated you well?"

You don't want to know the answer to that.

"Who is this man?"

"Bryant Meadows, Keeden's friend," she said, mentioning Keeden's name to give herself a small advantage.

Her parents were quiet for a long moment before her mother said, "I see," then fell silent.

Cat seized on the moment and said, "You're not losing me. I can still help out at the stores and I will make sure to train someone else to take care of your needs. I've made some calculations and you can afford—"

"I don't wish to discuss money right now." Her mother crossed her legs. "Fine, you can marry this man, but not for another five or seven years."

"That's too long."

"What is the rush?" She narrowed her eyes. "Is there a rush?"

"No, but we wish to marry within a year at least."

"Very well."

But she didn't believe her mother's calm response. She'd seen it before. Her mother wasn't going to accept losing her prized daughter. There would be a price to pay.

The price showed itself a week later.

In the form of a bright, red sock.

42

———

COME QUICK. *It's your dad.*

Bryant stared at the text from Gareth wondering if it was a hoax. He called to confirm. "What's—"

"I can't explain it," Gareth said in a rush. "We're doing our best but you've got to come now. We're in the laundry room."

"Help! Help! My son!" He heard his father shouting in the background. "They're killing my son! They're killing him!"

"He's in the corner and we can't get him to stop. And—"

"It's going to be okay," Bryant said, recognizing one of his dad's full on panic attacks. He kept his voice calm. "I need you to cover him with a large sheet or blanket, don't ask why just do it. Cover his head, tell him to close his eyes and recite a poem. It focuses his mind and gets him to breathe. Also touch his calf muscle and squeeze it, gently, it helps him. I'm on my way."

By the time Bryant arrived, his father wasn't shouting anymore, but he sat in the corner with a paisley sheet over his head mumbling something he couldn't understand.

Gareth rushed over to him. "I don't know what happened.

But we were taking the clothes out of the washer machine to dry and..." He motioned to the opened machine.

Immediately, he saw the destruction. All of his father's beautiful white shirts, spilled out of the front load washer like the dripping red tongue of a monster.

Bryant picked up one of the ruined shirts and recognized it as the one he'd bought his father for Christmas.

"I found this," Gareth said, pointing to the red sock he'd placed on top of the washer.

Bryant tossed the shirt back in the washer. "Just one?"

"Just one."

But one had been enough to turn all the shirts a garish pink.

To anyone else it wouldn't have mattered, but years ago his father had the same reaction when he'd dropped ketchup on his shirt. Once Bryant had managed to calm him down, his father admitted that any shade of red on his shirt reminded him of Bryant's blood. That day in Georgia his shirt had been covered in it.

But his father didn't wear red socks? How had someone managed to trigger this? Why would somebody want to? Had someone mistaken his load for theirs? But then why only *one* sock?

He patted Gareth on the arm. "I'm glad you were here. I'm going to take my dad back to his apartment. I need you put these in a bag."

"Want me to get rid of them?"

"No, I want to look at them later." He didn't like saying the words, felt like he was gathering evidence from a crime scene, but something felt off. He would find out what.

"Okay." Gareth began pushing the shirts back into the machine. "I'll wait until you walk him out."

"Thanks." Bryant walked to the huddled form in the corner and knelt in front of his father. "Dad? It's Bryant."

"My son."

"Yes," he said taking off the sheet and revealing his father's tear stained face. "It's okay. I'm okay. Come on."

His eyes darted to the washer machine. "My shirts—"

"We managed to salvage some," he lied. "Gareth will make sure to put them in the dryer and then you can iron them. You trust Gareth, don't you?" he asked helping his father to his feet.

"Yes, he's a good young man."

"Then let's go."

His father nodded and let him lead him away.

It took tea and biscuits to truly get his father to stop fretting about his shirts. Once Bryant had convinced him to have a lie down, Bryant went into the hall and called Keeden.

The moment his friend picked up he said, "I need a favor."

A visit from Uncle Martin rarely boded well. It wasn't because Cat didn't like the man, but his visits usually came with an agenda. Cat found him sitting at the kitchen table munching on a mandarin orange one late afternoon.

"I didn't know you were stopping by," she said. "What are you doing here?"

"Helping Mom spread the news," he said, aggrieved. "I told her it would be easier doing a video chat, but *no* she has to go to each and every house—"

"What news?"

His brows shot up. "You haven't heard?"

"Heard what?"

"I thought Maya would have told you."

"Told me what?"

"About Bryant."

Cat fell into a chair and stared at him. "What about Bryant? Is he okay?"

Uncle Martin popped a mandarin slice in his mouth before he jerked his head towards the living room. "If you want details you'd better get it from Mom. I'm staying here."

Cat left the kitchen her heart picking up pace as she headed down the hall. The closer she got to the living room she overheard words such as "Bound to happen" and "What a shame."

Cat entered the living room and greeted her grandfather's former lover, a nurse with pinched features and a body of voluptuous curves, before she said, "Uncle Martin told me something's happened?"

The two women shared a look before the nurse said, "Well, you know that I have a sister who works at the assisted living facility off of Winchel Road..." She then went on to explain her sister's routine and the weather for that day and a host of other details Cat didn't care to know. Cat rubbed her hands on her lap, trying her best not to appear impatient, hoping the woman would soon get to the vital point of her story since it would be poor manners to interrupt her. "...and then she was near the laundry room and heard such a fuss."

Cat blinked when the woman stopped at the most crucial part. "What fuss? What happened?"

"The man was completely batty."

Cat's mother sniffed. "Everyone knows that man needs special care. If that young man took better care of his father, it wouldn't have happened I'm sure. But he'd been distracted." She sent Cat a significant look. "Something like this was inevitable."

It was her mother's gaze, as well as her words, that turned Cat's heart to ice. Her mother was behind whatever had happened. She had orchestrated it all, but Cat couldn't accuse her in front of company.

Cat gripped her hands into fist, feeling her patience unraveling. "Will you please explain exactly what happened? Is Mr. Meadows okay?"

"Of course he's okay," the nurse said. "Such a silly thing to get upset about. His laundry was ruined by a red sock or some such nonsense. My sister said he screamed like a wounded animal. Poor man."

"Poor son," Cat mother's added with a click of her tongue.

"So true. What woman would want to marry a man with such a burden? I'd never let a daughter of mine saddle herself with such a person."

"Nor would I," her mother said with a soft, superior smile.

Cat quickly excused herself and raced to her room. She texted and called Bryant but received no reply so she called Maya.

"What is this about Mr. Meadows laundry?"

Maya told her about the ruined shirts.

Cat softly swore. Mr. Meadows' beautiful white shirts were like his old friends. It would shock him to see them destroyed. "How bad is he?"

"Things have calmed down. Keeden's out buying new shirts just so that Bryant has something to put in the closet and I'm doing my best to see what I can get online but some of the styles are no longer made. Keeden said he hadn't heard Bryant sound this desperate in a long time."

"I don't know what to do. I'm not sure I should go see him or stay away."

"I think they'd both like to see you."

"I'm not sure I should."

"Why not?"

"Because I think..." Her mind flashed to a receipt for a pair of red socks she'd never seen her mother or father wear, the fact that her mother knew about Mr. Meadows fragile state of mind, that she had connections to the facility too (she knew of three friends who had clients there), but most of all, her mother had a reason to cause Bryant trouble. "I think Mom might be behind it."

"Why would you think that?"

Cat told her about her engagement to Bryant and the conversation that had followed with her parents and all her suspicions. She waited for her sister to tell her that she was off the mark. That their mother would never do such a thing, but instead Maya softly swore and said, "I wish I could help you, but I'd only make things worse. I'm truly sorry."

"What should I do?"

Her sister sounded sad. "I can't tell you what to do, but whatever you do is going to hurt."

43

I NEED YOU.

Three words that had Cat swearing at every stoplight as she drove to Bryant's house after receiving his text.

She needed him too. She needed to see him. To see if his father was alright.

When Bryant opened the front door, Cat couldn't read his expression and when he spoke his words sounded oddly distant and polite. Did he suspect her mother too? Was he angry at her? She wouldn't blame him. She held up the food container in her hand. "I brought something for you to heat up later."

"You can put it in the kitchen," Bryant said before he turned and disappeared into the living room.

Cat swallowed. Bryant was definitely upset.

She went to the kitchen and placed the food in the fridge then closed the door and pressed her forehead against the hard, cool surface. She didn't know how she could fix this. If she should even try.

She walked into the living room and saw Bryant sitting on

the sofa with his hands covering his face. She cautiously sat down beside him and rubbed his back.

He dropped his hands to his lap. "I'm sorry I haven't been able to respond to your calls or texts," he said in the same polite, distant tone. "It's been difficult."

Difficult? Was that British understatement?

"I understand."

"After what happened in the laundry room, Dad had a lie down and I thought he was right as rain," Bryant said with an ironic chuckle, "then I heard him crying and he wouldn't stop, then he started talking about that awful day and I didn't want to leave him alone so..."

"You brought him home with you," Cat finished when he fell silent.

He nodded.

She waited for the questions. The accusations. But Bryant didn't move or say anything. He stared straight ahead looking at nothing in particular.

"How is he doing now?" she asked. "Do you want me to check on him?"

"No, not yet. He's resting. The worst is over."

She didn't know what to do, what to say. She wasn't good at comforting people and she wasn't sure that was what he wanted from her. Perhaps if she made some tea... No, Ovaltine might be better with something light to nibble on...

She stood ready to head to the kitchen but Bryant quietly said, "Please don't go yet."

She paused. "I wasn't...I won't. I'm not leaving." She sat back down and rubbed her hands together, uncertain. "What do you want me to do?"

Bryant turned and rested his forehead on her shoulder. "Nothing." He released a long, heavy sigh. "Sometimes I'm so tired. I want it to be over. I want him to be well again. I want to erase that day from our lives. I want to forget that it was my fault—"

"It wasn't your fault."

"If I hadn't worn that shirt—"

"It wasn't your fault and I'm sorry it happened."

"But—"

"I never take guilt trips and I avoid pity parties, so if you want me to stay you have to stop."

He sighed again and said in a grim tone, "I forgot that you're heartless."

"Yes, that's what you love about me."

He chuckled softly then wrapped his arms around her and held her tight. "Damn, you know me too well."

At first she didn't move, then she slid her arms around him too. She felt inadequate, feeling as awkward as an alpaca hugging a bear, but Bryant's restful sighs and steady breathing made her feel as if she was enough. "Have you eaten anything?"

"No."

"Then I think you and your dad could do with a good meal."

His father beamed with joy when he saw her. She instructed the two men to set the table while she heated up the food.

She pointedly ignored the angry ringing of her mobile, multiple calls from her mother, and blissfully prepared dinner. When her phone started to alert her to a series of text, she turned it off. She would deal with the consequences later. She wouldn't miss this chance to be with them one last time.

It was a dinner she'd remember—Mr. Meadows complimenting her on the yellow rice and black beans, Bryant feigning hurt that his father never complimented his food, them both laughing at Cat's imitation of her mother and sisters.

After dinner, Bryant's father returned to his room to read and Cat began to clean up the kitchen before Bryant brushed her aside. "You cooked. I can clean."

Cat folded her arms and leaned against the counter. "I think your father should move in with you."

"I was thinking about that too," he said, placing a washed dish on the drying rack. "But I wanted to discuss it with you first. I thought after we're married—"

"I can't...marry you. It's too much of a risk."

He turned sharply to her. "A risk?"

Cat hesitated then said, "I knew there'd be a consequence, but I never expected something like this."

Bryant pulled off his gloves and set them aside. "What are you talking about?"

"What happened to your dad. I don't think it was an accident."

Bryant folded his arms. "Go on."

"I think my mother was behind it. Don't ask me how I know, I just do."

He took a deep breath. "You really think she'd go that far?"

"Yes."

"If I talk to her—"

"No, you can't do that," Cat said near panic. "You don't know what she's really like. Few people do. But this is only the beginning. I'm so sorry." *Please don't hate me.* "I should have warned you about how she can...I should never have thought..." Cat shook her head. "I was being selfish, I thought maybe she'd let me... I'd never thought what we had would last forever. I fooled myself that it could."

Bryant stood beside her and lowered his head. Not in defeat or resignation, but in rage.

Cat swallowed, feeling the intensity of it. "Bet you wish you had a shovel and some soft ground right about now."

Her attempt at humor seemed to only anger him more. Bryant briefly closed his eyes before he glared at the countertop again, trailing his finger back and forth against it.

He couldn't even look at her. Not that she could blame him. What her mother had done to his beloved father was unforgivable. He probably never wanted to see her again.

She didn't know how to comfort him but she did know how to protect him.

Staying away was the best way to keep him and his father safe.

"I really am sorry you had to go through this. But my mother can be cruel. I've seen how she can treat people. She's patient and she'll strike when you least expect it, in ways you can't imagine. I could never protect my sister Maya. When she was banished from the family house I was relieved.

"And if banishment was also my fate, I would take it. I would take my mother's anger, her shouting curses and insults. I'd risk it all for the chance to marry you. But I won't sit back and watch my mother's poison infect your life. Or hurt anyone you care about. This stops now. With us."

He didn't look up at her. He kept rubbing an invisible spot on the counter.

Cat walked towards the pantry and reached for her apron.

"Leave it," a dark voice said.

She snatched her hand back as if he'd struck her. "I only wanted to—"

"I said leave it."

She wasn't one to cry, but her eyes burned with unshed tears, feeling the sting of his disdain. He didn't want her to leave with even the tiniest memento. He'd probably burn it.

"Say goodbye to your dad for me," she said. She expected no reply and didn't receive one.

Her heart felt like a boulder in her chest as she walked out the front door, surrendering to the icy grip of the night's cold chill.

BRYANT STILL DIDN'T LOOK up after he heard the front door close.

He kept trailing an invisible line, back and forth, with his forefinger. The rhythm helping to keep his temper in check.

Fury threatened to choke him.

He'd never heard Cat scared before. Never heard fear in her voice. The note of desperation. The nervous laughter. Never seen panic in her gaze.

It was strange seeing Cat scared.

But he wasn't scared.

Not. At. All.

What her mother had done should have scared him, but Mrs. Kayode had underestimated him.

Not only because of how she'd treated his father, but because of Cat.

He thought of her as a little girl running away. She hadn't told him all the reasons, he didn't believe it was because the house was crowded and no one noticed her. He suspected a deeper, darker reason that would drive a child to run away in an unfamiliar place.

This stops now. With us.

Yes, that woman's hold would end, with them. Bryant planned to make sure.

He wouldn't let Cat sacrifice herself.

He wouldn't let her mother keep them apart.

Bryant flattened his hand on the cold countertop.

Mrs. Kayode had started a battle he intended to win.

44

———————

"IT'S HOPELESS," Keeden said, sketching at one of the work stations in his large studio.

Bryant glared at his friend from his position on the couch. "I didn't come to you to hear that."

"I'm being honest." Keeden set his charcoal pencil down and spun his chair to face him. "She's put you in an impossible bind."

Bryant clapped his hands. "Your ability to state the obvious is amazing."

"I don't know what you want me to say. You know how much seniority and status are very important in our culture. You can't publicly shame or disrespect her, although she deserves both, without grave consequences. I don't think Cat wants to be responsible for that."

"I know."

"Are you sure Cat's worth it?"

Bryant sent him a venomous look.

Keeden held up his hands in surrender. "I'm just making a

statement. Mrs. Kayode is a scary woman and we both know you hate being scared."

"She doesn't scare me."

Keeden sniffed. "Then you're one of the few."

"Why aren't you worried about having her as a mother-in-law?"

"I have hundreds of years of history on my side. She wouldn't dare upset me."

"Lucky."

"I know. Unfortunately, I can't stop her hurting Maya in many different ways and I doubt you can save Cat. You can't win this woman over. It's not about her not liking you. So you can't charm her in any way. It's about Cat. She doesn't want you to have her. She doesn't want anyone to have her. That's what Maya told me."

"And Maya doesn't think there's any way..."

"You could move in with them."

Bryant stretched out his legs and stared at his shoes. "I'm going to pretend you didn't say that."

"Cat's right, it's not going to get easier. She won't let go."

"I'll have to find a way to force her hand."

"Without shaming or disrespecting her."

He sighed. "Right."

"There might be one way."

Bryant looked up, hopeful. "What?"

Keeden grimaced. "It's a little desperate and you won't like it."

"Try me."

~

BRYANT DIDN'T like Keeden's suggestion. In fact he hated it, but he was desperate enough to give it a go.

Two days later he found himself somewhere he thought he'd never be again: In a large hospital in Georgia. Fortunately, this time, he sat in the cafeteria not in a hospital room.

"What is this about?" the cardio-thoracic surgeon said, taking a seat in front of him. The V-neck sweater she wore complimented her delicately carved, West African features and her pressed black hair was pulled back into a neat bun. He noticed tiny streaks of grey which gave her an air of sophistication. "I'm busy. I really liked your suggestions about the bra's design by the way."

"Thanks."

"The team has made excellent progress on the flexible, washable circuits that will go with it. Women-focused health tech is the future and I've managed to secure more funding so we can—"

"Mum, I didn't come here to talk about business."

"Oh. Right."

"I'm getting married."

"Yes, I know," she said with as much interest as if he'd told her he'd bought a new tie. "Your father told me. Don't look so surprised. We still talk, although the conversations are mercifully short. He says she's very nice, but of course he says that about everyone." She paused. "Oh God, I hope you're not asking me to approve of her or something."

"No. It's her mother. She's a bit of a problem. She's Yoruba."

"So what?"

"I thought perhaps because you're also Yoruba you could—"

His mother started to laugh. "I could what? Speak to her in

our mother tongue and convince her to be nice to you? Don't be daft. If you can't handle her I suggest you end things now. It won't get better. Why would you want to marry a woman who can't handle her own mother anyway?"

"It's not that simple. If you let me explain the situation, maybe you could talk to her mother to mother and—"

"Out of the question. From what you've told me it's a waste of time and you know I hate wasting time."

Bryant took a deep breath. "I know, I only thought—"

"I don't think you were thinking at all. But that's just like you. All emotion and no sense. Don't look at me like that. This isn't a crisis. I'm shocked you'd fly all the way down here to discuss this. It wouldn't be the first time you broke off an engagement."

"I don't want to break this off."

"Then marry her and deal with a monster-in-law. It's your decision. I mean what did you really expect me to say?"

"I don't know."

Her brows shot up. "You don't know? You called me here for no reason?"

No reason. That's what seeing him again amounted to. Finding out he was getting married didn't impress her. She didn't even care to know more about Cat. He'd been wrong to reach out to her. Somehow he'd hoped she'd care enough to want to help him, to stand up for him against Mrs. Kayode. She had the status, the presence, the connections, she could have put pressure on Cat's mother if she'd wanted to. It might not have changed everything, but it could have done some good, make him and his father appear less like outsiders. They were still easy targets. Bryant banked down his disappointed. "I'm sorry."

"Well, it's not a complete lost. I'm still glad you're here.

You and I are doing something important. We're working on a device that could save lives. At least now I can tell you about the progress I've made…"

45

IT'S HOPELESS.

Why would you marry a woman who can't handle her own mother?

All emotion and no sense.

You cannot shame or disrespect her.

My mother can be cruel.

Bryant laid on his couch, staring up at the ceiling while his father laughed at an old sitcom on the TV he'd watched numerous times. It was one of his father's favorites about a despicably arrogant black British chef.

Absently Bryant overheard the actor, Lenny Henry, giving someone a scathing, well-targeted insult and wished he could do the same.

Nobody could help him, he was on his own. It'd been nearly three weeks since he'd spoken to Cat. He'd gone through many different scenarios of how he could deal with her mother but every idea either shamed her, disrespected her or both, which he most preferred but knew Cat wouldn't.

He felt useless.

"I think Cat should come live with us before the wedding," his father said.

I'm not sure they'll be a wedding. "Why's that?"

"She's not eating properly."

Bryant sat up and stared at him. "How would you know that?"

"When I saw her last week she hardly touched her cream puff."

Bryant froze trying to process two things at once. What? What! His father had seen Cat? And she'd left a cream puff untouched? A woman who could probably consume an entire chicken by herself wasn't eating?

The thought of her being so miserable that she couldn't eat made him feel sick.

"And she kept apologizing to me. I don't know why."

Kidnapping her was out of the question. There were laws against that.

"Oh, and I keep forgetting." He dug into his trouser pocket. "She wanted me to give you this." His father handed him a sleeping panda keychain.

Maybe kidnapping her was an option.

Bryant closed his hand around Cat's gift. "She said she'd stay away," he mumbled, "why was she doing this?"

"I know why you're both so unhappy."

"You do?"

"Yes, it's because of her parents, correct?"

How would he know that? "Yes."

"They don't want you to get married yet."

Bryant nodded intrigued by his father's insight. "That's right. But how—"

His father clapped his hands together in triumph. "That's what I thought! And I have a solution."

His Dad had a solution?

"I've been thinking about it for a while now," his father said in an excited tone. "Cat is the youngest and her family has already married off a daughter and soon another. Money must be tight and they probably want you to have a long engagement. A couple years perhaps?" His father didn't give him a chance to respond. "So I thought I could cover all the expenses so that her family wouldn't have to worry. It would be my gift to you. To both of you." He met his son's gaze. "You two belong together and she belongs with us."

Bryant sat speechless, stunned by his father's generosity. He never imagined there'd be a day when his father's innocence made him so happy.

Bryant closed his eyes against tears. He'd forgotten he wasn't alone. His father had always been there for him.

He hadn't lost his father that day, he'd gotten a different version of him. One he loved and who loved him back. Who always believed in him and wanted the best for him. He filled the space his mother couldn't.

He opened his eyes and gazed down at the keychain. "Thanks."

"Tell her tomorrow then invite her over for dinner. There's something I want to show her."

He couldn't tell his father the truth.

But he didn't want to disappoint him either.

Cat belongs with us.

You can't shame her or disrespect her.

Bryant glanced at the TV screen and saw a waitress place a plate of food in front of a patron.

Soon a devious, yet simple, idea began to form in his mind.

One that wouldn't shame or disrespect, but would work perfectly.

46

———

SHE MISSED him so much she'd started hallucinating.

There was no way Bryant could be outside her house, on a cold winter afternoon, tapping on the kitchen window.

Cat blinked expecting the specter of him to disappear. She didn't have time to start seeing things. She had a house full of guests set to arrive in about twenty minutes and platters of food she still had to organize.

She took a deep breath and returned to removing a tray of stuffed mushrooms from the oven.

The tapping grew more insistent.

"Cat, it's me."

Audio hallucinations as well? She crossed the kitchen and opened the window just to make sure. She gasped when his cold hand covered hers. He was definitely real. "What are you—"

"Open the front door." He walked away before she could reply.

She hurried to the front door and swung it open. "What are you doing here?"

His dark gaze swept over her, he was a man on a mission, out for blood. She never would have thought his anger would still be this intense. "Where's your mother?"

"Upstairs. I thought we'd agreed—"

"I need to talk to her."

He didn't look like a man who wanted to talk at all, instead he looked like he'd take pleasure in wrapping his hands around her mother's neck. She had to calm him down.

"The panda keychain was a peace offering. Didn't your father show you?"

"Yes, but it's not enough."

Her heart fell. Of course it wasn't. "You can talk to her later. Now is not a good time. I've got a lot of things to do and—"

His jaw twitched in anger. "So you're happily slaving in the kitchen for her again."

Cat placed a hand on his chest, desperate to get him to understand. "No, it's not that. Bryant stop." But he wouldn't stop. He kept walking, pushing her backwards, her slippers sliding against the hardwood floor like a mop. She jumped to the side and grabbed his wrist, but he only dragged her along with him towards the kitchen.

Then he halted and stared.

Cat shook her head. "It's not what you think."

"What am I supposed to think?" he asked looking at the display of food.

"I've got everything under control. I stood up to my mother. I always thought she was stronger than me. But the moment I faced her, I realized it wasn't true..."

~

Cat remembered seeing The List left on her desk as if nothing had changed. She remembered walking to the living room where her mother was enjoying a Nollywood drama and holding up the paper. She remembered the look on her mother's face—the surprise, the disbelief—as Cat slowly tore the paper in two. Then she tore it again and again until it resembled confetti, which she threw in the air. "From now on, I'll only cook for you if you pay me," she said.

Her mother sneered. "You don't mean that."

"Watch me." She turned and then felt a painful whack behind the legs that forced her to her knees. Her mother placed a viselike grip on her shoulder and held her down.

"Not you," she muttered in a low ominous voice. "I may have lost one daughter to Maya but I will not lose another."

Cat shook her head. "Maya has nothing to do with this."

"Our family was perfect—happy—before she came."

"No, it wasn't."

Her mother's grip tightened, her nails biting into Cat's flesh, causing her to wince. "It was. It *was*."

"Mom—"

"I will not let you disrespect me. Not you." She stood behind a kneeling Cat and held her down with both hands. "You were one of the ugliest babies I'd ever seen. I had to lie when visitors came to see you. Most times I'd cover you with a blanket and tell them you were sleeping so that no one would see you. And look at you now. You still have no looks to speak of and you own nothing!"

Cat remained quiet. The 'ugliest baby' story had been one her mother had repeated multiple times. Especially that spring in Georgia when her mother laughed uproariously every time she retold it to relations and strangers within Cat's hearing. Cat, who'd been taken out of school (only her, none of her sisters) on her mother's whim because she proved useful, the one who no one expected much from. It was a painful, hurtful tale that made her wish she'd truly been invisible so that she didn't have to feel the ache of being unloved. It had been one of the main reasons she'd decided to run away.

"You are nothing without us," her mother continued. "You need us. You think running to a man will save you? You think your life will be better with him?" She sniffed. "He'll never be true to you. Don't believe his lies. He doesn't love you. He'll have you looking after his father while another woman warms his bed. I know the world better than you do. I know what men are like. No man could love you as much as your family loves you."

Cat gritted her teeth against the pain surging through her knees, the burning ache of her shoulders, as her mother used the full strength of her body to hold her down. Her mother was physically stronger than she was, but her mother could not hold her down forever. At one point she would have to let go. The final tie had been severed. Her soul felt free.

Cat began to laugh. "You call this love?"

Her mother abruptly let go and stumbled back, surprised by Cat's reaction. "This is all Maya's fault."

Cat glanced over her shoulder. "This has nothing to do with Maya." She crawled over to the couch and used it to lift herself into a seat, not trusting her legs to hold her. "Why do you hate her so much?"

"I don't—"

"Yes, you do. Why? All my life I've seen it. We all have. It's not a secret how you feel about her even though she's done nothing to you."

"Nothing!" she said in a nasty tone. "She takes everything away. People always love her more than they love me. You and

Ava treated her like a mother more than you ever did me. She even stole my own mother's love. That girl just takes, takes, takes. She takes what should be mine."

Cat blinked, stunned by her mother's words. "No, she doesn't. She gives love in a way you can't. That's what really bothers you."

"No, it's that she turns the people I care about against me. Look at you." Her mother's voice trembled, tears glistened in her eyes. "It shouldn't be this way between us. It wouldn't be if... How can you look at me like that? I have given you my all. I have not withheld anything from you. Why would you treat me this way? I trust you. What am I to do without you?"

"I won't abandon you. I've said that before, but I won't live like this anymore."

"But to charge me—"

"Yes, because what you did to Bryant and Mr. Meadows was unforgiveable..."

"...so my mother is literally paying for what she did," Cat explained to Bryant in an abridged version of the past as they stood in the kitchen. "I told her that I'll only do two events a month and gave her the figures of how much that will cost. She will pay dearly for what she did."

Bryant walked over to the sink and washed his hands.

"What about the price you're paying?"

"Price?"

He dried his hands on the tea towel. "What's your worth?"

"My worth? I don't understand."

He sighed a little sad. "I know." He placed the stuffed mushrooms on a serving platter.

She placed cellophane over one of the platters glad for the help. "Oh, do you mean how much money I've raised? Well, I've only started so it's not much—"

"I'm not talking about money." He sent her a sharp look. "I don't need money. I have plenty of my own."

She felt helpless. He was taking away the one thing she thought she could offer him: Revenge.

"I know I'll never be able to win you back and I understand why you're still angry with me—"

Bryant shook his head before he checked the oven. "I was never angry with you."

Cat stared at him confused. "But you wouldn't let me take the apron."

"Exactly." He grabbed an oven mitt and pulled out another tray of stuffed mushroom and set it on the stove.

"Because you didn't want me to have it."

"No," he said in a soft voice, "because I didn't want you to take it."

"Right. And I know you're here because you want to see my mother punished but—"

He turned to her. "I didn't come here to punish your mother. I came here to rescue you."

"Rescue me?"

"You sound surprised."

"I am. I know you're angry, you can't pretend you're not. And if you hadn't gotten involved with me your father wouldn't have suffered. *You* wouldn't have suffered."

"Do you think loving you deserves punishment?"

"Loving me?"

He nodded.

It was a hard question to answer, an unnerving one. It dealt with feelings and thoughts she'd never considered before.

She'd always thought of herself as likeable rather than love-able and even that was a stretch, she didn't care much. She did now. Cat saw the price Maya paid for loving her. She didn't want Bryant to experience the same.

She gently nudged him aside, eager to change the topic. "Thanks for helping out here, but I really don't have time to talk anymore."

He fell quiet for a moment then said, "You still don't know your worth."

"I do," Cat said losing patience, "That's why I'm making my mother pay. I have to make up for—"

"Nothing. You don't have to make up for anything. I'm keeping the apron for my wife. And that person will be you. That's why I didn't let you take it with you." Bryant shook his head in amazement. "When will you understand how much I love you?"

Cat hid her emotions behind humor. "Well, according to my mother, that's impossible."

"Do you think it's impossible?"

"These stuffed mushrooms—"

"Answer me, Cat."

"I'm scared to believe it," she said, lowering her gaze to the counter. "My mother could wear you down so much that one day you'll regret—"

"Your mother doesn't scare me. What scares me is the thought that you prefer sacrificing yourself because you don't really want to spend your life with me. That you don't have the courage to tell me that living with my father—"

She lifted her gaze to his face, stunned. "No, no, that's not it. I love your dad. I want to prepare Ovaltine and shortbread cookies for him, and threaten to buy him a series of brightly colored kaftans, I want to scold you when you don't let the food simmer long enough, and hog your big screen TV, and tell you about my latest performance while we both sit on the couch and eat puff puffs and I want—"

His mouth covered hers and she succumbed to the pleasure of his lips, his warm embrace before he pulled away and his gaze bathed her in the strength of his love as he said, "Then you will have that and more."

Cat's lips burned from his kiss and her heart rejoiced at his words.

Her mother's voice broke through her reverie. "Cat, have you finished—" Her mother stopped and stared at the sight of them.

Bryant kept his gaze on Cat's face and mouthed, I can still rescue you.

I'm okay, she mouthed back.

"I'll see you tonight," he said aloud.

Her mother spoke up. "Tonight's impossible. You can see her tomorrow."

Bryant ignored her, his gaze never leaving Cat's face. "And I'll make breakfast."

"I can't," Cat said.

He narrowed his eyes his silent question asking, Why not?

Cat bit her lip then said in a quiet voice, "Baby steps. Try to be patient. I haven't cut ties with her completely. I promised to help clean up, but I can see you tomorrow."

Bryant's jaw tightened then he softly said, "I can stay and help you."

"I don't trust you."

"Why not?"

"Because you look like you want to slice my mother to bits and use her as garden fertilizer."

He shook his head. "I'd be afraid she'd poison the soil."

Cat giggled. "See what I mean?"

"You have a point. I should go. Convince me not to take you with me."

"Cat," her mother demanded, "the guests will be arriving soon."

"I can handle her," Cat said quickly, seeing a flash of fire enter his gaze.

"I can crush her," Bryant said. "Then she'll never frighten you again."

Cat bit her lip, amused by the flash of contempt that marred Bryant's face before he schooled his features again. "I don't want you to do that," she said. "Pretend to be nice, you're good at that." She kissed him on the cheek and whispered, "Goodbye, Death-Hunter."

He took a deep breath, before he said, "Promise me we'll come up with another plan that isn't this." He let his gaze sweep through the kitchen. "And if you ever get scared, you hold on to me."

"I promise."

He released her, satisfied and started to leave, but stopped beside Mrs. Kayode, who was standing in the kitchen doorway, and said with quiet warning, "I don't care about shaming you. I know the truth about your cooking. Push me too far and so will everyone else," before he bowed his head and walked away.

47

———

"Are your eyes closed?"

"Yes," Cat said as she let Mr. Meadows lead her up the stairs.

They'd barely finished dinner before he'd jumped up from the table and said he had to show her something.

Once she reached the landing and headed down the hall, she heard a door open and Bryant sharply inhale his breath.

"You can open them now," his father said.

Cat slowly did then gasped. She saw a mannequin draped in a beautiful, but sleek outfit made of exquisite lace and hand woven decorative fabric with a matching gele. The outfit wasn't showy and spectacular; its beauty lay in how simple and elegant it was.

"Gareth helped me set this up," he said with pride.

"You were buying the cloth for me?" she said, feeling as if she'd fallen into a strange fairy tale.

He walked over to the orange and red dress. "It's for your wedding day." He sent an anxious glance at his son. "You told her I'll pay for everything, right?"

Bryant shoved his hands in his pockets. "I haven't gotten around to that."

His father returned his gaze to her. "But I will. You don't have to worry about anything." He lightly touched the sleeve of the dress. "Do you like it? I know I'm not the best tailor."

She lightly touched a sleeve. She'd never be a beautiful bride but she'd certainly be an interesting one, which suited her perfectly. "You sewed this yourself?"

He nodded. "Long ago I took a sewing course at the center and I've been practicing." He rubbed the back of his neck embarrassed. "And I got some help from a neighbor when I got stuck, but I did most of it myself."

"This must have taken months," Cat said in awe. "It's more than I could have ever dreamed. I don't know what to say."

He walked over to Bryant and nudged him towards her. "Say you'll love him even though he's not perfect."

Bryant turned sharply to his father, "Dad."

Cat smiled and felt her heart melt at the older man's sweet gaze as he offered her his son, his most treasured gift. Her own father had never looked at her with such love and tenderness.

She remembered the lost, sad nine year old she'd been and the friendly gentleman who'd waved at her. Who'd noticed her.

She never would have imagined following him would lead her here—lead her home.

She hugged him and whispered, "I will."

EPILOGUE

Cat inhaled the scent of curried rice as she passed one of the sampling stalls at World Foods. She'd stopped by the liquor store to visit with Vanessa and had been unable to resist the urge to quickly pop in to see what was available.

But if she wasn't careful she'd get into trouble and spend more than she needed to—again.

Although she no longer received The List anymore (her mother no longer hosted events at the frequency she used to and used the excuse of family obligations and grandchildren as a reason why she hadn't managed to cook in a while) Cat still bought more food than her household needed.

Even hosting frequent visits with Gareth and his grandmother, Vanessa and her brother, her sisters and their spouses and The Old Woman, wasn't enough to curb her habit.

But she would be good this time. She glanced down at the hand basket she carried (at least it wasn't a cart) that only held three items (and not fourteen which she'd managed to squeeze in before). She promised herself only one more item before she left.

It wasn't her week for cooking dinner (she and Bryant alternated), but she still wanted to test out a new recipe.

She'd negotiated a paid part-time position managing inventory at her parents' cloth store and also continued to help run their household—hiring and dealing with different contractors and housecleaners, making sure any extra expense remained within their budget. Things were working well so far, although her parents refused to say so and made a pointed effort not to attend her wedding.

She hadn't missed them.

Cat left the condiments aisle and stopped when she saw the back of a tall, familiar figure that looked as if he'd been pulled from a fashion spring catalog dressed in khakis and a light green linen shirt. He examined items in the Produce section.

She wondered if Bryant's meeting with Gareth had ended sooner than he'd expected and he was killing time. He'd invested in the younger man's simulation game idea. It was designed to help seniors and those who cared for (or about) them to practice avoiding scams and how to identify the various disguises they came in.

Gareth also maintained a popular site where he and Bryant's father shared tips and advice on the subject. Mr. Meadows made sure to wear a pressed white shirt for their weekly video chats and their friendship continued to deepen every day. Fortunately, after another heartbreak (a rogue who actually stole her jewelry and pawned it), his grandmother had decided to take a break from finding a new love and focus on the friendships she'd made through her new swing and salsa lessons.

The word 'salsa' turned Cat's mind from dancing to food. She thought about the delicious avocado peach salsa that Bryant had added to their breakfast of scrambled eggs and crispy potatoes.

She licked her lips in fond memory. Was that why he was looking at the avocados? Or did he plan to make something else?

She crept up behind her husband, curious for answers. "What are you going to make?"

He jumped and the avocado slipped from his hand and landed on the pile. He frowned at her. "I wish you wouldn't sneak up on me like that."

She playfully poked him in the back. "It's too much fun to resist."

He glanced at her hand basket. "What are you buying?"

She hid the basket behind her. "Nothing."

"You're too skinny to try to hide anything. I doubt you could conceal a piece of string."

She made a face. "Oh, thanks," she said in a sour tone, pulling the basket forward. She sighed. "There are only three things."

"Hmm," he said then added them to his basket.

She grinned, pleased he was willing to pay for them without argument. "Thanks."

He returned his attention to the avocados.

"Oh, I keep forgetting," Cat said folding her arms. "Keeden once told me to ask you about your angel."

Bryant paused. Then he did something he'd never done before—something genuine and real. He slowly turned to her and smiled.

ABOUT THE AUTHOR

Dara Girard, an award-winning, national bestselling author of more than fifty novels, from romance to suspense, loves telling stories.

Born in the US to immigrant parents, Dara enjoys pulling from her Jamaican, British, Nigerian heritage and exposure to various cultures to bring what reviewers and fans call "vivid emotional stories" to life. She is best known for her popular Henson Series, the mysterious Clifton Sisters, and the fun Black Stockings Society.

You can write her at:
contactdara@daragirard.com
or
ILORI Press Books
c/o Dara Girard
P.O. Box 10332
Silver Spring, MD 20914
If you'd like to receive a reply, please send a self-addressed stamped envelope.

Visit her website to sign up for her newsletter and get sneak peeks, monthly updates on new releases, and special offers.

www.ingramcontent.com/pod-product-compliance
Lightning Source LLC
Chambersburg PA
CBHW061803190726
48289CB00007B/2052